WARTIME

WARTIME

Stephen James Walker

First published in Great Britain by
Telos Publishing Ltd 2023

This paperback edition published 2025

ISBN 978 1 84583 211 7

Contents

Foreword
Keith Barnfather

What does *Wartime* mean to me? It's a question I've been asking myself a lot lately, as the publication of this novelisation has drawn closer.

From the day I formed Reeltime Pictures in 1984, the idea of making a drama based around my favourite television series was churning in the back of my mind. After a few failed attempts negotiating with the BBC, I realised the only way we would move forward was to simply secure rights *not* held by the BBC and go ahead!

So in 1986, that's exactly what we did. I say *we* because this was always a collaborative effort by a group of frustrated, creative individuals ... who also happened to be fans. Looking now at the list of names involved ... John Ainsworth, Mark Ayres, Nicholas Briggs Andy Lane, Helen Stirling ... they all progressed to successful careers in 'the business'.

The production team were all learning their trades and we made mistakes ... but the love, enthusiasm and determination we had to finish the production saw us through and we came out of it having learnt so very much. We had virtually no budget ... but what we achieved over the five days location filming was (and still is) truly amazing.

Then there were the lead actors, John Levene and Michael Wisher, who both took an incredible risk in taking part ... especially John, who cared a great deal for Benton and knew he was risking the integrity of the character. I shall forever be indebted to them both.

What does *Wartime* mean to me? Everything. I think I forged my career during its making. It gave me confidence and a desire to do more ... much more. Reeltime Pictures will celebrate its 40th anniversary in 2024 with countless productions 'under its belt', including award winning dramas and documentaries.

My very grateful thanks to David J Howe and Stephen James Walker of Telos Publishing for being so supportive of Reeltime over the years ... the publication of our dramas as novelisations has been something I've derived great pleasure from. I'm especially grateful to Stephen for so sensitively expanding *Wartime* and tying it into the series of Reeltime's Earth-based dramas ... read on and you might see what I mean ...

Keith Barnfather, Producer
Reeltime Pictures
November 2022

During the late 1960s, the United Nations, acting on a series of highly classified reports, formed a secret global taskforce.

Its brief was to investigate the increasing number of incidents involving the abnormal, the unexplained, the dangerous. In fact anything on Earth ... and beyond.

Its name: the United Nations Intelligence Taskforce.

UNIT recruited specialists from every field. One of these was John Benton.

Not all Benton's work was for UNIT.

Sometimes it was closer to home.

1
The Mission

London, Friday 10 October 1990

'Wait here, would you, please, Mr Benton?'

Benton thanked the pretty young official, whose name he hadn't caught, and she quickly withdrew, closing the door behind her.

He had been shown into a small, functional meeting room furnished only with a table and chairs, a smaller side-table bearing a coffee pot and cups and, at one end, a whiteboard on a stand. There were no windows – this was deep in the interior of MI6's Thameside headquarters – and the only illumination was provided by a single ceiling strip-light, giving the place a distinctly claustrophobic feel. Benton took a seat at the table, but couldn't get comfortable. He was like a fish out of water here, and felt strangely awkward wearing his military uniform in a building full of civil servants. Over the last decade or so, he'd got more used to being in civvies himself, assigned by UNIT to one undercover operation after another. He remembered an incident when, posing as a used-car salesman, he'd —

His wandering thoughts were brought abruptly back to the present as the door opened and two men entered. The first, who looked to be in his early fifties, close to Benton's own age, wore a dark suit and tie and a pair of thick-rimmed spectacles, and carried a sheaf of papers under one arm. 'Good morning. I'm Edward Baker,' he said.

Benton rose quickly to shake the proffered hand, getting his feet tangled up in the chair-legs in the process.

Baker indicated the other, more casually-dressed man, clearly his junior, both in age and in status. 'This is Martin Carter,' he said. 'He'll be taking notes.'

'Can I get you a coffee?' asked Carter, gesturing to the side-table.

'Oh, no, thank you,' Benton replied. He'd tasted Civil Service coffee before.

Baker and Carter sat down on the opposite side of the table to Benton, and he resumed his own seat. Then, pleasantries disposed of, Baker spread out his sheaf of papers and began the formal business of the briefing.

'You'll be familiar with the situation in the Middle East, of course,' he said.

Benton fingered his collar nervously. Global politics wasn't exactly his strong suit. 'Well, since the Iraqis invaded Kuwait ...' he ventured.

'Just so,' said Baker, with a brief nod of his head. 'With Operation Desert Shield now ramping up, we in the intelligence community are naturally facing significant and pressing demands on our resources. One of the many tasks with which we've been charged is seeking to identify sites where the Iraqis might be secreting WMDs.'

On military matters, Benton was on firmer ground. 'Weapons of mass destruction,' he muttered.

'Indeed. Of course, we're heavily reliant on

analysing surveillance data from satellites – military and civilian – although we also receive reports from our covert operatives there on the ground in Iraq.'

Baker paused to select a particular folder from within the papers in front of him. He opened it and pulled out three small black-and-white prints.

'These satellite images,' he continued, 'show some kind of excavation site, in the desert about 135 miles from Basra.'

He passed the prints across the table to Benton, who flicked through them uncertainly, screwing his eyes up to try to make out some detail in what appeared to be a small group of black blobs in the middle of an expanse of grey sand. 'These are about as clear as my dear old aunt's holiday snaps!' he said.

Carter, the notetaker, quickly stifled a chuckle as his superior shot him a stern look.

'They're not ideal, I admit,' Baker replied, in what seemed to Benton a rather defensive tone. 'But still clear enough for us to judge that whatever's being buried there – or perhaps dug up – resembles no sort of weapons system with which we're familiar. And that's not all ...' He paused, as if almost embarrassed by what he had to say next.

'Go on,' prompted Benton, thinking that at last they were getting to the crux of the matter, and that he might now find out exactly why he was being temporarily seconded to the Security Intelligence Service.

'Well ...' Baker went on, 'reports from one of our informants amongst the local Kurdish revolutionaries suggest that there's something distinctly ... odd ... going on at that excavation.

There's talk that whatever they've got there might not be a weapons system at all. That it might be something ... alien. Perhaps even some kind of crashed alien spaceship ...'

'So, you put in a call to UNIT,' nodded Benton.

'Well, you are the experts in that sort of thing,' Baker acknowledged. 'I suppose, it being an international matter, we should strictly speaking have gone via your high command in Geneva, but as I'm sure you'll know, Britain's relations with the UN are not what they once were ... and, given all the sensitivities around our forces' participation in Operation Desert Shield, we'd rather keep this within the family, so to speak. At least for the time being.'

Benton shrugged. Politics again. 'All I know is, I've got my orders: to assist you to the best of my abilities in whatever mission you assign me to.'

'Ah, yes, the mission,' said Baker, selecting another document from amongst his papers. 'I have to tell you frankly, Mr Benton, that I give very little credence to these fanciful "alien spaceship" stories. Personally, I think what we're dealing with here is probably a cache of some newly-developed kind of WMD that we've not encountered before. But, be that as it may, we do need to find out exactly what's going on there. So, we're sending in a small team of SAS men on a stealth reconnaissance mission; and we want you to go with them, as a specialist adviser, just in case they do find anything ... out of the ordinary.'

With this, he handed the document over to Benton, who scanned it with an experienced eye.

'That gives you all the basic information you'll

need,' Baker told him. 'You're to report tomorrow morning to the SAS training facility in the Brecon Beacons, where you'll be given a more detailed briefing and some basic training to prepare you for the conditions out there in the Iraqi desert. Any questions?'

'I don't think so,' Benton replied, rising to his feet. 'This all looks pretty comprehensive.'

'Yes, I think we've covered everything,' said Baker.

'Oh, except,' chipped in Carter, with a grin, 'don't forget to pack some sunscreen. It's hot out there!'

2
The Dig Site

The Iraqi Desert, Saturday 25 October 1990

Lying flat on his front on the coarse sand of the Iraqi desert, eerily bathed in the light of the almost full moon high overhead, Benton ruefully recalled Carter's words of only a fortnight earlier. It had indeed been swelteringly hot during the day, as they had made their way stealthily over the border from Saudi Arabia and across the desert in a pair of camouflaged Desert Patrol Vehicles – DPVs for short – led unerringly toward their destination by their two Kurdish guides; but now, in the dead of night, it was distinctly chilly. Unnaturally so, in fact. Benton knew from his advance briefing that the night-time temperature here rarely dipped below 20°C at this time of year, but he reckoned it was closer to 10°C currently. Like a crisp autumn day back home. He'd encountered freak weather conditions a few times before on UNIT missions, so he had a shrewd idea what the cause was. The dune on which they had hunkered down was at the top of a low ridge affording an excellent elevated view of the dig site that he had previously seen only in MI6's blurry satellite photos, and that he was now convinced must be harbouring one or more alien artefacts of some kind.

He glanced across at the three similarly prone SAS officers to whom he had been assigned: Ollie 'Spadger' Hughes, Doug 'Frosty' Frost and Dan 'Ratto' McPhail. He knew that they had all been somewhat suspicious of him when he was first introduced to them at the Brecon Beacons training camp. Theirs was a close-knit group and he was an interloper. More than that, they had evidently doubted his fitness to accompany them on this mission; not unreasonably so, Benton had to acknowledge, as he was all too aware that these elite military men – supremely fit, highly trained, rigorously professional – were barely more than half his age. In fact, he strongly suspected that the intensive preparatory training exercises he had been put through back at the camp, some of them undertaken in simulated desert conditions inside a huge hangar-like building, had actually been more for their benefit than for his, to give them some reassurance that he really would be able to cope with the punishing conditions they were likely to encounter in Iraq. Fortunately, he had always kept himself in shape, and although it had cost him more effort than he cared to admit, he had completed all of the exercises successfully, earning him their grudging respect. You had to be made of tough stuff to survive a long career as a UNIT operative.

Their small team was now alone in the desert: the two guides, Seyyed and Ali, had insisted on remaining a couple of kilometres farther back, keeping watch over the DPVs until their return; a display of caution that the others put down to superstitious fear on the Kurds' part, but that Benton felt was probably wiser than they realised. The three

SAS men now had their eyes fixed intently on the dig site below, scanning the area with compact night-vision binoculars. Spadger, the team leader, gave Benton a nudge and handed him a pair of the binoculars.

'Have a look down there,' he murmured. 'See what you think.'

Benton put the twin lenses to his eyes and peered down at the object of their mission. Unlike in the satellite photos, the central area of the site was now almost obscured by a large tarpaulin that had been suspended above it, draped at roughly head height over a kind of crude wooden support frame. Around this were parked, rather haphazardly, several earth-moving machines – a bulldozer, a couple of excavators and a dumper truck – and two or three light armoured vehicles. Stationed around the perimeter of the site were about half-a-dozen men attired in the uniform of Saddam Hussein's Revolutionary Guard.

At first Benton thought that everything looked pretty much as one might have expected, with nothing out of the ordinary. As he studied the scene more closely, though, he started to realise that there was something not quite right about it. A little beyond the array of stationary earth-moving equipment he could see a smaller vehicle, a fork-lift truck, but this was far from stationary: it was spinning round and round at high speed, as if completely out of control, even though he could just make out the shadowy figure of an operator in the driver's seat. Benton's immediate reaction was to wonder why the nearby guards were not rushing to the operator's aid; but when he focused the binoculars on them, he could see that most of them were slumped listlessly at their posts, while one of their number had dropped to his knees in an attitude of prayer, and another was bizarrely spinning round and round like a whirling dervish, as if emulating the fork-lift's movements.

Benton scratched his head in puzzlement. 'What the hell's going on down there?' he wondered aloud.

'They must be high on drugs,' said Ratto, with characteristic bluntness.

'Maybe their water's been spiked by our guides' Kurdish chums, or something?' suggested Frosty.

Benton lowered the binoculars and rubbed a hand across his eyes. Staring at those colour-drained night-vision images was starting to give him a headache. 'No, that's not it,' he replied. 'I think they're being affected by whatever it is they've uncovered in that dig.'

'What ... like radiation?' queried Spadger.

'Could be,' agreed Benton. 'Or some other type of energy. Or maybe they've been sent doolally by some kind of ... mental influence.'

The SAS men exchanged glances, and even in the moonlight Benton could discern the scepticism in their expressions.

'I've seen that kind of thing before,' he insisted, 'when there's alien gubbins involved.'

'Well, you're the expert,' said Spadger, doubtfully.

'I'm just guessing, mind you,' Benton admitted. 'What we really need here,' he added under his breath, 'is a scientific adviser.'

'So,' hissed Ratto, 'what are we waiting for? They've obviously gone nuts. Who cares why?

Now's our chance to get down there and find out what's under that tarpaulin.'

'Yeah, and deal with it,' added Frosty.

Benton shot him a sharp look. 'What do you mean, "deal with it"?'

'Well,' cut in Spadger smoothly, 'if it is a stash of WMDs they're trying to conceal, we're not just going to walk away and leave them there. We're going to do whatever we can to disable them – put them out of action.' Grinning, he added: 'And if you're right about it being something … alien … I guess we'll just have to play things by ear!'

Ratto and Frosty shared a chuckle at this, and Benton was keenly aware that his comrades still weren't taking entirely seriously the possibility of there being otherworldly artefacts down in the dig. But he trusted he could count on their professionalism regardless.

Raising the binoculars to his eyes again and taking another look at the site, Benton saw that the guard who previously had been kneeling as if in prayer was now running about wildly, tearing at his own clothes. 'My god, look at that …' he muttered, shaking his head in astonishment.

'What do you say, then?' pressed Spadger.

'Well, we do need to get into the site and take a proper look at it,' Benton acknowledged. 'It's what we came here to do. But even if those guards give us no trouble, the state they're in, we'll still need to keep our wits about us: just bear in mind, whatever's affected them could affect us too.'

'I think we'll cope,' said Ratto dismissively.

'But let's not get over-confident, eh?' cautioned Spadger; and for the first time, Benton saw a flicker of anxiety cross the man's face.

Frosty was still studying the extraordinary scene below through his binoculars. 'This is … worrying,' he acknowledged.

Coming to a decision, Spadger continued more positively: 'Okay, no time like the present. Let's get going.'

When they had first arrived at the ridge, the three SAS men had set down the heavy bergens they had hefted on their backs on the arduous walk across the desert sand from the DPVs, but now they stashed away the binoculars and shouldered the packs once again, checking them over with practised hands. Benton felt slightly guilty, but at the same time relieved, that in his role as a consultant he had not been expected to carry any equipment himself. He had, though, been supplied with a handgun, and was pleased to feel its reassuring weight resting in its holster against his hip.

At a sign from Spadger, all four men crawled over the lip of the dune and began moving in a crouch toward the dig below, half walking and half sliding down the sandy ridge. Benton made sure to keep pace with the others. His headache was getting worse, and he had to admit to himself that he was deeply apprehensive about what the next few minutes might bring. It hadn't escaped his notice, either, that the closer they got to their objective, the colder it was becoming, as if all the heat was being sucked out of the air somehow. He recalled experiencing something similar, many years earlier, in the Devil's End incident, and was fervently hoping that this wasn't going to be as bad as that.

When they got to the bottom of the ridge and

were just metres away from the site, Spadger motioned the others to follow him in single file in an anticlockwise direction around the perimeter. Benton immediately realised what he had in mind: to skirt around to where the earth-moving machines were positioned and use those for cover as they moved further in, so that they could get as close as possible to the central tarpaulined area without being detected. Fortunately, their stealthy advance was aided by the fact that, although there were lighting rigs fixed to pylons at regular intervals around the site, all directed inward toward the centre, none of them was working; the only illumination, aside from the natural moonlight, came in the form of a sickly green glow emanating from under the tarpaulin itself.

The downside of Spadger's plan was that in order to reach the small cluster of earth-moving machines they had to pass close to the nearby fork-lift truck, which was still spinning round and round in a tight circle, carving out deep ruts in the sand beneath its wheels. It wasn't just his throbbing headache that caused Benton to feel a wave of nausea as, despite the dimness of the light, he caught a clear glimpse of the vehicle's Iraqi operator. The skeletally-thin figure was hunched forward in the driver's seat, his arms outstretched stiffly in front of him and his hands clamped tightly onto the controls, holding them in fixed positions. But the worst thing of all was his face, which was contorted in a terrible rictus, his eyes bulging almost out of their sockets and thin ribbons of drool running down his chin. How long he had been sitting there, maintaining that same rigid posture within the furiously spinning vehicle,

Benton didn't care to speculate; doubtless he would keep it up until his body finally gave out, or at least until the fork-lift's battery did.

Thankfully, this gruesome sight was quickly obscured from Benton's vision as the team took cover behind the solid bulk of the nearest excavator. From there, they proceeded to make their way cautiously forward, weaving a path between the parked machines, until they reached the one closest to the centre of the site. A little farther on from this they spotted a stack of metal crates previously hidden from their view by the earth-movers. At a gesture from Spadger, they crept forward again and took up a new position behind this convenient barrier, crouching low down on the sand. Glancing at the crates, Benton was at first a little alarmed to see that they all had yellow radiation hazard symbols affixed to them. Then, though, he noticed that some of those at the top of the stack had their lids lying open and were totally empty. If the Iraqis were indeed burying WMDs here, as the SAS men thought, then this could be how they had been brought onto the site; but if, as he himself believed, they were actually digging up alien artefacts of some kind, then the crates could be standing ready to transport them away.

Even though the four men had now infiltrated deep into the site, they still couldn't quite make out what was in the very centre, shaded from the moonlight by the tarpaulin roughly slung above it. The green glow seeping out from under the tarpaulin should have been enough to give them a reasonable view, but somehow it just seemed to confuse their senses, casting weird shadows everywhere; and, to make matters worse, there was a faint shimmer in the air, rather like a heat haze – although it was actually very cold now. Benton thought he could just detect a glint of light coming from a silvery metal structure on the ground, but he couldn't be entirely sure.

The short distance from the stack of crates to the tarpaulined area seemed completely clear, and Spadger was just about to wave the team onward to their goal when Ratto reached out and caught him by the arm.

'Wait a second,' hissed Ratto. 'I … I thought I saw someone moving about over there, just by the edge of the tarpaulin.'

Everyone peered into the semi-darkness, trying to see what he had seen.

'I think you might be right,' said Frosty.

Spadger, though, was sceptical. 'I can't see anything. It's probably just those strange shadows.'

'I saw someone, I tell you!' insisted Ratto, becoming agitated now. Suddenly he stood bolt upright, a shocked expression on his face. 'My god … it's my boyfriend!'

'What in hell's name are you talking about!' demanded Spadger, as Benton and Frosty shared a look of sheer bewilderment.

'It's my boyfriend! I can see him clearly now!' said Ratto, smiling broadly.

'This is no time to start clowning about!' fumed Spadger. 'And for god's sake keep your voice down!'

Seemingly oblivious, Ratto abandoned the cover of the stack of crates and began walking rapidly toward where he said he had seen the figure. Spadger reacted without hesitation, recklessly rushing after Ratto and rugby-tackling him to the ground. Hampered as they were by their heavy bergens, the two men nevertheless proceeded to grapple with each other, their violent thrashing movements throwing up small showers of sand all around them, as Ratto repeatedly screeched, 'Get off me! Let me go!'

Frosty instinctively made to head off after his two comrades, to try to break up the fight, but Benton held him back. 'Hold on, Frosty. There's no way the guards aren't going to hear that godawful racket they're making. If any of them are still thinking straight, we're going to be in big trouble.'

Benton could see that Frosty was caught in two minds; but eventually he nodded in agreement. 'What do you think we should do?'

'Well,' said Benton, with a deep breath, 'if we really want to find out what's under that tarpaulin, this is probably our last chance. I know it goes against the grain, but if the guards do come running, they're going to have their hands full with Spadger and Ratto, and that should give us a few minutes' grace.'

Frosty thought about this for only a moment before once again nodding in agreement. They really had no choice.

'Okay,' said Benton. 'Let's do it.'

At that, the two men set off at a run, bypassing the still wrestling figures of Spadger and Ratto and quickly ducking under the edge of the tarpaulin.

Finally, they had reached the dig itself, and Benton swiftly surveyed the scene. The top layer of sand had been cleared away here in a wide arc to uncover not far below the surface – it seemed the excavators had hardly been used yet – the silvery metal structure he thought he had glimpsed earlier. Circular in shape, and tilted at a slight angle, it was without doubt a spaceship, albeit a small one; perhaps – what was the phrase? – an escape pod, ejected from a larger craft. A cantilevered rectangular hatch at the top was thrown back, and a series of dents along one side of it suggested that it had probably been forced open. A tangle of wires and cables snaked out from this entry point and across the sand to a bank of instrument panels positioned around the sides, and Benton guessed that Iraqi scientists must have been using these to take readings and measurements of various kinds. But it appeared that none of the instruments was operational now; the panels were lifeless, with not a single screen or bulb lit up.

As Benton's eyes grew more accustomed to the gloom, he noticed other dents and areas of damage across the spaceship's hull, though whether these were further examples of the Iraqis' handiwork or whether they had been caused during the ship's landing, or even before that, he couldn't say. But it was the open hatch that was the source of the lurid green glow that afforded the area's only illumination. The light seemed to be radiating out from a semi-transparent dome that sat just below the rectangular opening, and as Benton studied this dome more closely, he thought he could see something moving about within it. The writhing shape, bathed in its sickly green light, had a kind of hypnotic effect on him, and his headache grew even worse. Managing with an effort to tear his eyes away from the ship, he saw that Frosty was similarly transfixed. He shook him by the shoulder.

'Snap out of it, Frosty! We've got work to do. We need to shoot some video of this, record as much of it as we can, for the science bods back home.'

'What?' replied Frosty, in a dazed voice.

'The night-vision camera – there should be one in your bergen. We need it now!'

With ponderous, trance-like movements, Frosty slowly unshouldered the bergen and laid it down on the sand, all the time keeping his eyes firmly fixed on the ship. Benton was just about to grab the bergen and start searching within it for the camera when, without the slightest warning, all hell broke loose.

Sudden shots rang out as one of the Iraqi guardsmen – judging by the terrible state of his uniform, the one that Benton had earlier seen tearing at his own clothes – rushed into the tarpaulined area, firing his rifle completely at random, with a manic grin spread across his face. Before Benton and Frosty had time to react, the man had barrelled into them, almost knocking them off their feet, still firing wildly in all directions. They tried frantically to restrain him – thankfully the attack had shocked Frosty out of his state of torpor – but he seemed to have the strength of a man possessed.

As focused as he was on the struggle, it did not escape Benton's hearing when two short, sharp bursts of gunfire sounded farther off – the noise coming, he realised grimly, from the direction of the stack of crates where they had left Spadger and Ratto tussling on the ground. He had no time to worry about that now though.

Eventually, with Frosty's help, Benton managed to wrench the rifle from their assailant's grasp before either of them was hit by a stray bullet. His relief was short-lived, though, as he saw with alarm that the man was now reaching for a grenade hung from a loop on his belt. Fortunately Frosty had also spotted this new danger, and together they redoubled their attempts to subdue the Iraqi.

Their efforts were in vain. Hard though they tried to keep the man's arms pinioned, he soon broke free from them and, with a triumphant cry, seized the grenade. Then, still gripping the compact device tightly in his hand, he pulled the pin.

In a final act of desperation, Benton and Frosty grabbed the guard and flung him bodily away from them, sending him flying through the air and crashing into one of the banks of scientific instruments, which collapsed under his weight, sending up a shower of electrical sparks. Benton and Frosty meanwhile dived for the meagre cover of a low pile of sand, obviously discarded to one side when the Iraqis had been digging out the shallow pit around the spaceship.

Benton did not expect to survive the grenade blast. They just weren't far enough away from where the guardsman had fallen. When it came, though, the explosion was much less violent than he had expected. Had the grenade failed in some way? After a moment, he ventured a cautious look over the top of the pile of sand. Their Iraqi assailant had been blown to pieces by the blast, but Benton's attention was mercifully distracted from this stomach-churning sight by the fact that floating in the air around the remains of the man's body was what looked like a shimmering sphere of dazzling white light. For a moment Benton was mystified, but then it dawned on him that the main force of the explosion had somehow been contained within this sphere, as if frozen in time. As he watched, one edge of the sphere bulged outwards, extruding a thin funnel of light that snaked its way through the air and then through the spaceship's open hatchway, where it connected with the dome beneath. The sphere then gradually faded away, as the energy from the explosion was drawn down the funnel and into the dome.

Abruptly the dome slid open, and from within rose up what was unmistakably an alien creature. Roughly humanoid in form, the pale green figure had a small body, with thin, withered-looking limbs, and a large, bulbous, hairless head. Set in a row of shallow indentations across the otherwise featureless face were four tiny, lidless eyes that blazed like hot coals.

Benton got slowly to his feet, climbed over the pile of sand and advanced a few steps toward the creature, which seemed to be hovering in mid-air just above the ship, its body haloed by a green glow. He was almost mesmerised by the sight, but nevertheless took in the fact that the creature appeared to be injured: down the right-hand side of its body it had a deep gash, from which oozed a dark-green fluid, and its right arm hung limp and motionless. Perhaps it had been trying to heal itself by syphoning off energy from its surroundings – which would explain the anomalous low temperature and the non-functional lights around the site – and the detonation of the grenade had supplied enough for it to be at least partially revived? That was Benton's guess, at any rate.

He was just about to try talking to the creature when suddenly someone leapt on him from behind and clamped an arm viciously across his throat. At first he thought this must be another of the Iraqi guards, but that assumption was quickly disproved as, twisting around to try to free himself, he saw that his attacker was actually Frosty.

'What the hell are you doing?' he croaked.

'You bastard!' shouted Frosty. 'You betrayed us to the enemy! We should never have trusted you!'

The SAS man had a wild, crazy-eyed expression on his face, and Benton knew that to try to reason with him would be futile: he was completely out of his mind.

The lack of air reaching his lungs, coupled with his throbbing headache, was making it difficult for Benton to think straight, but of one thing he was in no doubt: it was the creature's malign mental influence that was responsible for Frosty's derangement, as it had been for the incapacitation of the Iraqi guards. He looked round toward the creature, and saw that its four burning eyes were all focused directly on him, staring at him balefully.

There was only one thing for it: abandoning his instinctive efforts to wrest Frosty's arm from around his throat, Benton reached down, drew his handgun from its holster and, taking aim as steadily as he could in the circumstances, fired off a volley of shots at the creature. Most of the bullets missed their mark, but one struck the alien directly in the centre of its chest, and immediately it slumped forward and fell to the hull of its ship, the green glow around its body waning. For a moment Benton was hopeful that he had managed to kill it, but then his hope faded as he saw that it was still moving, its good left arm twitching feebly: evidently he had failed. The pressure of Frosty's arm around his throat was unrelenting, and he felt consciousness gradually slipping away from him.

Suddenly another shot rang out, and instantly Frosty released his grip on Benton's throat and collapsed to the ground, blood coursing from a bullet hole right above his heart. Benton could scarcely believe what had happened. Doubled over in pain, his chest heaving as he sucked in great lungfuls of the cold air, he looked round to find out where the shot had come from, and was amazed to see the moonlit figure of Spadger limping toward him across the sand from the edge of the tarpaulin.

'I thought you were dead!' he wheezed.

Spadger shook his head. 'Can't get rid of me that easy,' he said, returning his handgun to its holster. 'Just picked up a little flesh wound, that's all,' he added, pointing to his hip.

'Is Ratto …?'

'Dead,' replied Spadger abruptly. 'It was either him or me,' he explained, a hint of guilt in his voice.

Remembering the brief burst of gunfire he had heard earlier, coming from beyond the tarpaulin, Benton chose not to question further. Doubtless neither Spadger nor Ratto had been in full possession of their senses at the time.

So astonished had Benton been by Spadger's unexpected arrival on the scene that he had been momentarily distracted from what was going on behind him. Realising his mistake, he wheeled round, expecting further trouble, but was relieved to see that the creature was now lying completely inert on the battered hull of its ship. It looked as lifeless as the prone form of Frosty splayed at Benton's feet. Although he took no great pleasure from the fact, apparently he had succeeded in killing it after all.

Spadger let out a low whistle as he took in the extraordinary scene before him: the crashed spaceship lying partly excavated in the shallow pit of sand; its alien pilot sprawled unmoving outside its open hatchway; and, a little farther away, just visible in the low light, the Iraqi guard's remains strewn across the wrecked bank of scientific apparatus.

The immediate danger over, Benton found that his thoughts were starting to clear. Making a conscious effort to pull himself together, and carefully averting his eyes from Frosty's bloodied body, he picked up the man's discarded bergen and began rummaging around inside it.

'What are you up to?' asked Spadger, who was no longer wearing his own bergen; presumably he had lost it during the fight with Ratto.

'Looking for the video camera,' Benton replied. 'You told me you each had one. We need to get all this on tape.'

'I'll tell you what else we each had,' said Spadger grimly. 'Explosives. We need to blow this place up, not waste our time videoing it.'

'It's no waste of time,' retorted Benton. 'We've got to collect as much intelligence as we can. For all we know, this could be the first sign of an alien invasion attempt.'

'I get that,' said Spadger, through gritted teeth, 'but if we're starting to think clearly again, maybe the guards are as well. Any minute now, we could find ourselves having to fight our way out of here.

We can't afford to hang about.'

So saying, he grabbed the bergen from Benton and began pulling out numerous stubby black cylinders from the bottom of it; obviously the explosives he'd mentioned.

'To tell the truth,' he went on, sounding a little abashed, 'this was never just a recce mission. The plan was always to blow the place up. Whether it was WMDs or alien artefacts, we weren't going to leave them in the Iraqis' hands; and we couldn't exactly take them back with us.'

Benton had to admit that Spadger was talking sense: their situation was distinctly perilous. But then a thought occurred to him. 'We can't take the spaceship back, obviously,' he said. 'But we can take the alien.'

Spadger regarded him as if he were mad. 'What are you talking about?'

'Look,' said Benton, 'you can set your explosives if you like, but I'm going to get that alien and put it in one of those metal crates we saw outside. Then, between us, we can carry it back to the DPVs. If you're up to it, that is,' he added, remembering that Spadger was wounded.

For a moment Spadger looked as if he was going to argue, but then he gave in: 'All right, if that's what you want. I'm up to it okay. But you'd better get a move on; I'm not going to take my time over this.'

Before Spadger had a chance to change his mind, Benton jumped down into the shallow pit, clambered up onto the hull of the spaceship and gently took the creature's limp body up into his arms. As he had hoped, its spindly form was not at all heavy; only its bulbous head lolled a little awkwardly as he made his way back down to the sand, cautiously watching his step to make sure that he didn't slip on the metal hull. Leaving Spadger to his work, he ran out of the tarpaulined area and across to the nearby stack of crates, carefully skirting around where the luckless Ratto had fallen. Reaching up, he then deposited the alien body in one of the open crates at the top of the stack, closed the lid and snapped the catches shut.

Benton hoped he might still have time to capture a little video of the spaceship, but when he turned to go back, he saw that Spadger was already emerging from under the tarpaulin and limping over to him as quickly as he could. Suddenly, though, Spadger stopped dead, pulled out his handgun from its holster and aimed it in Benton's direction.

Benton froze on the spot, thinking that Spadger must have relapsed into mental confusion. When the shot came, though, the bullet sped past his shoulder, and he heard a shriek of pain pierce the air behind him. Wheeling round, he saw one of the Iraqi guards collapsing to the sand, a rifle falling from his lifeless hands.

'I told you we couldn't afford to hang about,' said Spadger, as he came up to join Benton.

'Thanks,' was all Benton could say.

'No problem. But now we need to get out of here. I've set those explosives to detonate in five minutes.'

Spadger made to head off, but Benton caught him by the arm.

'Wait a minute. Help me with this crate.'

So saying, Benton took hold of the carrying handle at one end of the crate in which he'd placed the alien's body. With obvious reluctance, Spadger grasped the handle at the opposite end, and together they lifted the crate down from the top of the stack. Then, lugging it between them, they set off for the edge of the site.

This time they made no detour around the earth-moving machines. Instead, taking the risk of being seen, they went in the opposite direction, heading straight toward the low ridge from which they'd earlier observed the site. They needn't have worried: although they did pass close to one of the surviving Iraqi guards, the man was still slumped at his post, looking completely exhausted, and while he turned his head listlessly toward them, he made no effort to prevent their escape.

Ascending the ridge was a lot harder than descending it had been, particularly with the added burden of the crate and the impediment of Spadger's wounded hip. On the plus side, Spadger no longer had his heavy bergen to carry. They reached the top without further incident and threw themselves over it, into the hollow of the dune beyond. As they lay there on the sand, catching their breath, Spadger consulted his wristwatch.

'Any time now,' he said.

He was right: only a few moments later, a series of thunderous blasts reverberated behind them and a huge plume of fire and smoke lit up the night sky above the dig site.

Benton was surprised by the violence of the detonations; those explosive devices might have been small, but they certainly packed a big punch! He risked a look over the top of the ridge and saw that there was now just a large crater where the central tarpaulined area of the site had previously been – the spaceship must have been totally destroyed – while beyond that the bulky excavators had been scattered about like toys.

Spadger reached into his jacket pocket and pulled out a field radio. 'Seyyed and Ali will have heard those explosions,' he said. 'I need to let them know what's going on and warn them that we're on our way back. With any luck, they might be able to meet us part-way with the DPVs.' When he tried calling the Kurdish guides, though, to his obvious consternation he received no response at all.

There was nothing for it: the two men took up the crate once more and, using a compass to get their bearings, trudged off across the desert sand toward where they'd parted company with the guides, with no idea what they'd find when they got there.

Benton was greatly relieved when the rendezvous point finally came within view and he saw the reassuring silhouettes of the two camouflaged DPVs still parked exactly where they'd left them. Spadger had been finding it increasingly tough going as they'd laboured onward, gritting his teeth against the pain of his injury, and Benton had started to wonder if they were actually going to make it. His relief was tempered, though, by the fact that there was no sign at all of the two guides.

When at last they reached the DPVs and gratefully set the crate down on the sand, their worst fears were confirmed. They found Ali lying face down between the two vehicles, the back of his cream-coloured tunic soaked in bright red blood. Benton flipped the body over, and they saw that the man's chest was pierced by a row of bullet holes.

'Poor devil,' said Spadger, running his hand gently over Ali's face to close his wildly staring eyes. Quickly he scanned the area, alert for any danger. 'Where on earth is Seyyed?' he hissed.

His question was answered almost immediately as a low groan of pain came from beyond one of the DPVs. Hurrying round the rear of the vehicle, they discovered Seyyed sitting on the sand, propping himself up against the metal chassis, with blood running down one side of his forehead.

Benton rushed over and knelt by his side. 'You shouldn't try to move,' he cautioned. 'Are you badly hurt?'

'No, no,' replied Seyyed, waving away his concern. 'It's not as bad as it looks; just a graze. I'll be all right in a minute.'

'What the hell happened here?' demanded Spadger.

'We were taken by surprise,' said Seyyed. 'When our attention was distracted by those explosions. Two Iraqi guards rushed us, firing their rifles. They weren't really aiming, though; they were just shooting everywhere. Ali was unlucky, but I took cover here. I just got caught by a stray shot. Then they both ran off into the desert. It was like they were out of their minds.'

A frown of puzzlement creased Benton's face. He hadn't expected that the alien's insidious mental influence would extend so far from the dig site, or that it would persist even after it had been killed and the site destroyed. And, come to think of it, the neat row of bullet holes across poor Ali's chest seemed inconsistent with the idea of random firing. Something wasn't adding up here.

'Do you mean to say–?' he began; but Spadger placed a silencing hand on his arm.

'Look, Benton, we haven't time to hang around here and chat. We need to get going – particularly if there are rogue Iraqi guards running about.'

Benton would have liked to question Seyyed further, but he had to accept that Spadger had a point.

'Okay,' he said. 'Let's get the crate into the back of the DPV.' Turning to Seyyed, he added, 'You'd better come with us. We can get you to a first-aid post in Saudi Arabia.'

Seyyed shook his head. 'I told you,' he said, 'it's no more than a flesh wound. I just need a minute to recover from the shock, that's all. Then I'll head after you. We can't just abandon one of the DPVs here.'

Again Benton felt inclined to take issue with this, but Spadger had already resumed his grip on one of the crate's carrying handles and was waiting impatiently for him to take the other.

Leaving Seyyed hunched on the sand, leaning against the DPV, Benton and Spadger lifted the crate into the back of the second vehicle. Then, after helping Spadger into the passenger seat, Benton got in on the driver's side and started the engine.

With a brief salute of farewell to Seyyed, Benton swung the DPV around and sped off across the desert sand. They would have to find their own way back to Saudi Arabia, he knew, now that they had lost their guides, but he was confident they could retrace their route successfully. With any luck, he told himself, it would all be plain sailing from here on.

As soon as he was sure he was alone, Seyyed rose to his feet and climbed into the driver's seat of the remaining DPV. Grabbing a discarded rag, he used it to wipe his forehead clean.

'Thanks for the blood, Ali,' he muttered to himself. 'At least you were good for something.'

Then he put in a call on the vehicle's radio-telephone.

'There was a small problem,' he told his unseen contact. 'After we heard the explosions, Ali got nervous and started to make trouble, so I had to dispose of him. But two of the Englishmen survived, and they brought something back with them – carried in a metal crate – so I made an excuse and let them leave with it, just as you said.'

'Excellent,' came the satisfied reply. 'My agent can intercept the consignment when they get back to the UK.'

'Do you want me to continue watching the dig site?' Seyyed asked.

'No, there's no point now. You've done very well, Seyyed. I'll be in touch.'

With that, the call ended.

Seyyed started up the DPV, put it in gear and, grinning broadly, headed off in a direction well away from that taken by Benton and Spadger.

3
Phantoms

Lancashire, Monday 27 October 1990, Midday

The Land Rover sped along a tree-lined country road. In the passenger seat, Benton lifted the radio-telephone handset. Time to report in. 'Greyhound Four, over.'

'Ah, there you are, Benton. What's your current location?'

Benton allowed himself a brief smile as the Brigadier's voice came through loud and clear, unmistakable despite the hiss of radio static. This was almost like old times. Lethbridge-Stewart, called back into service yet again. Something to do with Merlin and Excalibur, he had said, though Benton thought that was probably just a joke. Would the man ever truly retire?

'Just outside Bolton, sir. Over.'

'How long will it take you to reach UNIT HQ? Over.'

'Well, hopefully about four hours, sir. I know these roads like the back of my hand. Over.'

Like the back of his hand. That was true. The covert early-morning landing that had delivered him and Spadger to the RAF Woodvale training facility just north of Liverpool – where he and the SAS man had parted company with a warm handshake after an uneventful flight back from Saudi Arabia – had meant that, as fate would have it, his route down to London was bringing him very close to his boyhood family home.

'Good,' approved the Brigadier. 'Any problems? Over.'

'We saw a car behind us sometime earlier, but I reckon it was just a coincidence, sir. Nothing now. Over.'

'Who's your driver? Over.'

Benton cast a glance at the combat-uniformed man sat alongside him in the driver's seat, his eyes focused on the road ahead.

'Willis, sir. Private Willis. Regular Army. Over.'

'Right, Benton. Be alert. Look after that shipment. Out.'

Shipment. Of course, that was why the Brig had asked who the driver was. He wouldn't want the regular Army man to be clued in to what was really inside the metal crate they were transporting in the back of the Land Rover.

'Yes, sir. We'll be careful with it.' With nothing further to report, Benton signed off. 'Greyhound Four, out.'

His confident tone masked the fact that he was feeling distinctly on edge. He was still deeply unsettled by the whole incident in Iraq, and had a strange sense of foreboding about this ostensibly routine drive down to London. Glancing in the wing-mirror, he saw that there was again another vehicle not far behind them. It looked like a Mercedes. Was it the same one they had spotted earlier? He couldn't be sure. Probably he was fretting over nothing, he told himself. After all, there was bound to be other traffic on the road at this time, in the middle of the day.

But his mission wasn't the only thing that was troubling him. It was this area, the memories it held for him.

They came to a T-junction and, glancing down at the map, Willis prepared to make a right-hand turn. Benton raised a hand to his temple. He had a headache coming on. The memories were strong here, very strong, and there was something he felt he just had to do.

'Go left,' he instructed.

The dark-haired young Private regarded him curiously. 'Are you sure, sir?'

'Yeah, this will only take a minute.'

Willis complied, swinging the Land Rover round to the left, onto a narrower, unmarked road, bordered here and there by low drystone walls.

As they drove along, Benton was uncomfortably aware that this brief unscheduled detour was strictly against orders. But surely it couldn't hurt, could it? He cast a glance over his shoulder at the metal crate lying under the canvas hood in the back of the Land Rover, and drew some comfort from the sight of the two bright yellow radiation hazard decals pasted across the top of the casing. Those surely should be enough to scare off any curious passers-by, shouldn't they? Looking up, he was further reassured to note that the other vehicle was no longer behind them; it must have taken the right-hand turn, back at the T-junction.

Returning his attention to the road ahead, he steeled himself to keep his gaze firmly fixed there. He really didn't want to look over to the left. He knew what he would see, if he did so. In the end, though, the urge became irresistible. And there it was, bleakly silhouetted against the clear blue autumn sky, atop a ridge in the middle distance: the Tower.

Mercifully, the road dipped a little just then, and the edifice disappeared from view behind some trees. A little farther along, Benton indicated to Willis to pull over, and the driver brought the vehicle to a stop in a safe spot at the side of the road. Benton got out and closed the door, which was emblazoned with the same distinctive circular UNIT logo as he wore on his cap-badge.

'Wait for me here,' he instructed. 'I won't be long.'

Willis, puzzled, leaned across in the driver's seat and called after his superior's rapidly-receding back: 'Sir! We've got to be at UNIT HQ by five!'

Benton, though, wasn't listening. He was striding away, seemingly in a world of his own.

'Sir! Where are you going?'

Passing through a metal-barred gate and ascending a flight of timeworn stone steps, Benton soon found himself exactly where he had known they would lead him: the forecourt of the local church, St Martin's. Proceeding more hesitantly now, he rounded the far corner of the building and entered the graveyard. It was a long time since he had last been here – too long, he reproached himself – but still he remembered just where to go. He approached the grave and knelt down on one knee in the unmown grass before it. To his surprise, he saw that someone had placed a single white rose in a flower-holder right in front of the headstone. Overcome with emotion, and with his headache growing worse, he had to stifle a sob. A jumble of painful memories was whirling through his mind: the Tower; his young brother, screaming and falling; his grieving parents … He had no need to read the inscription on the headstone – he knew it off by heart – but its central words stood out starkly: *Christopher Anthony Benton, 1939-1944, RIP*.

'Oh Chris,' he murmured, the words catching in his throat. 'I'm so sorry. I'm so sorry.'

He paused for a moment to run his fingers tenderly over the soft white petals of the solitary rose, then got to his feet again and walked slowly away. His head was spinning. It was almost as if he could sense Chris's ghostly presence there in the graveyard, his innocent, fair-haired young face peeping out from behind the headstone …

Benton shivered and quickened his pace, and in no time at all he was back at the Land Rover and taking his seat again beside the evidently unsettled Willis.

They resumed their journey, following a circular route that would eventually bring them back round to the correct road. But Willis's initial relief at Benton's return was short-lived, as he quickly realised that his superior was still acting strangely, sitting with his hands clasped to the sides of his head and his face contorted as if in pain.

Benton, for his part, was completely oblivious to the disquiet his odd behaviour was causing Willis, and indeed to everything else around him. His aching head was consumed by thoughts of the Tower, looming ominously on the ridge away to their left, and of the tragic significance it held for him and his family. He felt almost as if he was back there again now, as a child, together with Chris. He could recall their conversation with total clarity, like a recording replaying in his mind.

'Where are you going?' he asked his brother.

'To the old Tower,' Chris replied. 'Straight over there.'

'Mother will be angry,' he warned.

'Are you coming, or what?' was the defiant response.

Suddenly Benton was an adult again, sending a desperate but futile warning back into the past: 'No, Chris. No!'

Willis cast another anxious glance across at his superior. But his concern would have been greater still had he happened to check his rear-view mirror and seen that that same Mercedes car was now trailing them once again ...

If it wasn't one thing, it was another, reflected Willis ruefully. No sooner had RSM Benton regained his composure – thank heavens! – than the Land Rover's engine had started to play up, for no apparent reason. It was almost as if it was overheating, although it had been thoroughly checked over before they had set off, and this wasn't exactly a warm day. He recalled how, back at base, he had laughed when his fellow squaddies had teased him that, having been given a UNIT assignment, he was bound to experience some spooky stuff. Now, it didn't seem so funny after all.

As the engine finally died, Willis steered the Land Rover to the side of the road and brought it to rest by the grass verge under the shade of some overhanging trees. Then he got out and popped open the bonnet to see if he could find the source of the trouble. Benton also got out, retrieved his rifle from inside the vehicle and pulled back the bolt.

Willis looked up in surprise. 'Trouble, sir?'

'If there was going to be trouble, Willis, this is the spot I'd choose.'

Having quickly scanned the surrounding woodland and thankfully spotted nothing untoward, Benton reached in through the Land Rover's open window and tried turning the key in the ignition a couple of times. The engine spluttered, but refused to start.

A quick glance at the metal crate lying in the back of the vehicle was all that Benton needed to convince himself that he ought to report in to HQ with this troubling new development. He raised the radio-telephone handset to his mouth and spoke into it urgently.

'Greyhound Four to Trap One. Greyhound Four to Trap One. Do you read me? Over. Greyhound Four to Trap One. Greyhound Four to Trap One.'

Unexpectedly, and disturbingly, his words were met with complete silence.

'Come on, come on,' he muttered. 'What's wrong with them? Why don't they answer?'

Benton could feel his headache returning with a vengeance. He whirled round in alarm as suddenly he heard a noise like the dull thud of an explosion, off in the trees somewhere behind them. Surely that was a grenade, wasn't it? This damned headache! He couldn't think straight. All he could hear now, replaying in his mind, was the unheeded warning he had given his brother Chris, all those years ago: 'It's dangerous … It's dangerous …'

'Willis?' he called.

Willis broke off from his tinkering with the Land Rover's engine and came round to the rear of the vehicle, where he found Benton staring off into the trees.

'Sir?'

'Which direction did that come from?'

'Did what come from, sir?'

'The grenade, man, the grenade! Didn't you hear something?'

'No, sir.'

Benton's brow furrowed in puzzlement. How could Willis not have heard that noise?

'I'm going to check that out,' he told the young Private. 'Get the vehicle fixed. If I'm not back in ten minutes, get out of here.'

As Benton moved off into the woods, alert for any trouble, Willis prudently grabbed his own rifle from inside the Land Rover and placed it within easy reach before resuming his work under the bonnet. A smile of satisfaction crossed his face as, almost at once, he succeeded in getting the engine restarted. Maybe things were looking up! Benton's strange behaviour was still a concern, though, and he felt a headache coming on. He shut and secured the bonnet, blinking his eyes several times to try to clear them, as all at once he found he was having trouble focusing ...

Benton proceeded cautiously through the woods, holding his rifle at the ready and using the trees and undergrowth for cover. But he couldn't find the site of the explosion he had heard, and although he had the strangest sensation of being watched, the place seemed utterly deserted. Soon he found himself ascending a steep incline, and started to sweat a little from the exertion, although the air was positively chilly now. He took his cap off, rolled it up and put it in his pocket.

Eventually his path brought him to a semi-ruined stone bridge, and as he moved across it, a shiver of recognition ran down his spine. Suddenly he realised exactly where he was. This was Rivington Gardens, the once beautiful but now neglected Victorian park that he and his family had visited so often, back when he was a boy. Including on that fateful day when Chris had lost his life …

Benton shouldered his rifle, marvelling at the coincidence – it must be a coincidence, mustn't it? – that had seen the UNIT Land Rover break down so close to this old childhood haunt of his. All thoughts of his mission, and of the noise he felt sure he had heard, were pushed from his mind as he became consumed by memories – some happy, some traumatic – of those far-off wartime days.

Reaching the other side of the bridge, he made his way up a winding flight of uneven stone steps that brought him to a terrace where a small waterfall trickled into a pool bordered by verdant foliage. He paused briefly to rest in this tranquil setting, wishing his mind was as clear as the fresh, lightly rippling water of the pool; but he just couldn't shake off that nagging headache. He resumed his wandering through the park.

Before long he came to a clearing where there lay on the ground a distinctively-carved piece of fallen masonry that was immediately familiar to him. He went over to it and knelt beside it on the leaf-covered ground.

'How many times did we play here when we were

kids?' he murmured.

This had been a favourite spot for him and Chris to amuse themselves with games of hide-and-seek. He could almost see his younger brother crouching down there, covering his eyes and calling out, 'Nine, eight, seven, six, five, four, three, two, one. Coming!' Then Chris would race off to start searching.

He remembered how they had once chalked their initials on this piece of masonry, along with the date: *CB + JB 1944.* That had been on the very day when their horseplay had ended so tragically; when Chris had run over to the old Tower and he had chased after him, clambering up to where his young brother had perched himself so precariously on a narrow stone ledge. He could still hear Chris shouting, 'Johnnie! I can see you, Johnnie!', as he himself had reached up to try to catch him …

Benton spun around as suddenly he heard what sounded like a child's scream. Shouldering his rifle again, he set off running in the direction he thought it had come from, up another flight of weathered stone steps that led to a higher terrace. In the back of his headache-clouded mind, he was dimly aware that he was becoming confused, and that he couldn't be entirely sure whether he really had just heard a scream, or whether it was the terrible ingrained memory of Chris's own scream, all those years ago, as he had fallen from that ledge …

Back at the Land Rover, Willis was feeling no better, and was now experiencing a strange kind of double vision. When he looked around him, it was as if everything was moving in slow-motion. He lit a cigarette, hoping it would calm his nerves, and rested his back against the frame of the Land Rover's open door. Preoccupied as he was, he failed to notice that he was being watched from just a short distance away by a man who was standing partly hidden behind a tree. Nor was he aware of the man pulling a handgun from his jacket pocket and loading a bullet into the chamber …

Rifle levelled, Benton made his way cautiously down the far side of the terraced gardens, eventually reaching the outskirts of the woodland beyond. He hesitated there and scanned the sky as he thought he heard a plane passing overhead. Then came the muffled *crump* of several more explosions off in the distance, like a cluster of bombs falling. This time, though, he reacted more warily. He had the uncomfortable feeling that he was being deliberately lured farther and farther away from where he had left Willis and the Land Rover. Not only that, but he was no longer sure that he could fully trust his own perceptions. Looking down at his hands, he suddenly saw that he was holding not a rifle but a wooden stick.

'Somebody's playing games,' he muttered. 'And I don't like it at all.'

Flinging the stick away, he moved off again; not in the direction from which the explosions had seemed to come, but back into the park. His discarded rifle lay abandoned on the rocky patch of ground behind him …

Now, as if in direct response to his failure to follow the sound of the explosions, Benton's headache intensified dramatically, and with it his mental confusion. Glancing down into the murky water of a pond, he saw his face reflected back at him; but it was his face as a young boy, not as he was now.

'Bang, bang!' he heard his younger self shouting.

He continued on, retracing his steps over the tiered terraces, his head in a whirl. From the vantage point of a high stone-walled bridge, he looked down to the path below and saw two young boys – one fair-haired, one dark, both dressed in short grey trousers, white shirts and blue pullovers – having a mock swordfight with wooden sticks like the one he had just discarded. Was that really happening now, or was he simply remembering how he and Chris had once played? He just couldn't think straight.

Hurrying down the steps from the bridge, he went after the two boys, but briefly lost track of them after they split up and hared off in opposite directions through the overgrown gardens. Then he heard their voices again and caught sight of them chasing each other across the terrace immediately above the one on which he stood. 'Bang, bang, you're dead!' shouted the dark-haired boy, pointing his stick at the other like a gun.

Benton raced up another flight of steps, taking them two at a time, and finally caught up with the pair, who had sat down with their backs to him on a low stone circle at the top of a steep grassy bank.

'Stay there!' he demanded, scrambling up the bank behind them. 'I want to talk with you boys.'

But they completely ignored him – did they even hear him? he wondered – and, with a shout of

'Come on!', the fair-haired one was off again, eager to resume their game. The dark-haired one looked round briefly, and for a moment Benton thought the lad could see him.

'Who are you?' he demanded. 'Who are you?'

But the boy simply shrugged his shoulders and raced away after the other, still wielding his stick.

Benton rocked back on his heels, trying desperately to get his thoughts in order. He hadn't really needed to ask who the boys were. He no longer had any doubts on that score: the fair-haired one was Chris, and the dark-haired one was his own younger self. They were not real, but phantoms of the past.

He knew exactly where they were headed, too. The Pigeon Tower, it was called now, although it had had other names over the years, and to him and his brother it had been simply the Tower. A stone-walled edifice, some four storeys high, standing as a forbidding local landmark at the northern edge of Rivington Gardens. He recalled vividly in his mind's eye how, on that fateful day, Chris had climbed up the steps to the Tower, then up onto its walls, and how he had chased after him. Again he saw himself reaching up to where Chris was stood, teetering on that narrow ledge, with a sheer drop below.

He heard his brother's voice: 'Johnnie! I can see you, Johnnie!'

Then had come the fall, and that terrible scream.

Although he knew deep down that the scream wasn't real, was just a memory, Benton couldn't resist reacting to it. Quickly scaling a nearby wall, he scanned the horizon to try to see where it had come from.

'Chris!' he shouted desperately. 'Chris! Chris!'

Willis, still waiting back at the Land Rover, was now deeply concerned. He had been ordered to drive on if Benton hadn't returned within ten minutes, but he couldn't seem to work out how much time had actually passed. His head was killing him, and he couldn't shake off the strange sensation that everything was moving in slow motion …

Benton was dimly aware that he was gradually losing his grip on reality. As hard as he tried to fight it, his childhood memories were starting to overwhelm him, the present and the past becoming intertwined in his mind so that he could no longer distinguish between them.

Passing along another of the stone terraces, he thought he heard the faint sound of music playing somewhere nearby. Glancing up, he was astonished to see his parents, as they had looked back in wartime, dancing an elegant waltz across the bridge above, his mother in a smart pink dress with a string of pearls around her neck, his father in his Army uniform and also, bizarrely, his gas-mask.

'Mother! Father!' Benton called. But the couple showed no signs of having heard him; they just continued their strange dance, waltzing back and forth in each other's arms across the bridge, oblivious to all around them – until, suddenly, some unseen force seemed to pull them apart, and they both started to topple backwards, as again there came the distinctive thud of a nearby grenade explosion.

With an alarmed cry of 'No!', Benton bounded up the steps to the bridge. But when he got there, his parents had vanished. Instead, he found just a single white rose lying on the ground where they had been dancing. His brow furrowed in puzzlement. Surely that was the same rose he had seen earlier, on Chris's grave, wasn't it? He reached down to pick it up, caressing the petals as he had done before, but gasped as a thorn pierced his skin and blood ran down his hand. He threw the rose back to the ground.

Willis knew that longer than ten minutes must have passed by now since Benton had gone off into the woods – possibly much longer. But he knew also that, as things stood, he was in no fit state to drive the Land Rover. He must be having a migraine, he told himself – although that wasn't an affliction from which he usually suffered. All he could do was continue waiting, and hope that his headache and blurred vision would soon improve, or that Benton would return …

Benton raced up the steps toward the Tower. In his mind, he was a child again, chasing after his brother. 'Chris?' he called. 'Chris?'

'Come on, slowcoach!' came his brother's voice. 'Last one to the Tower's a sissy!'

'Chris, please wait!' he pleaded. He was really worried now. Their parents had warned them not to go as far as the Tower. It could be dangerous.

'Sissy!' came Chris's mocking reply.

'Where are you?' Benton demanded.

'Sissy!'

Benton was struck by a sudden idea. He would turn this into a game of hide-and-seek again. Maybe then Chris would stop running and give him a chance to catch up.

'Coming!' he called. 'Ready or not!'

'Sissy!' was all the response he got.

Benton had had enough of these taunts. Holding up both hands, with his fingers crossed in a time-honoured gesture of defence, he called: 'Pax, Chris! You can't touch me, I've got pax!'

Suddenly Chris appeared through an archway on the steps above, holding his stick out in front of him like a rifle. Benton started to move toward him, but then recoiled as another figure joined him on the steps. It was a stocky, dark-haired man in his late twenties, holding not a stick but a handgun. Benton was momentarily jolted back to the present as he recognised this man as the driver of the Mercedes he had seen following the Land Rover earlier on. Before he could say anything, though, the man fired the gun at him at point-blank range.

'Bang!' came Chris's triumphant shout, as Benton collapsed to the ground. 'You're dead!'

When Benton regained his senses, it was to the sight of the autumn leaves rustling in the trees above and his mother looking down at him solicitously, her face framed by her neatly-styled brunette hair. 'Afternoon, sleepyhead,' she said. 'Feeling better now?'

Benton sat up abruptly. 'What happened?' he demanded, bewildered. He saw that there was a picnic set out on a blanket on the ground, and relaxing around it were his mother, his father and Chris. His parents looked just as he had seen them earlier, dancing together on the bridge, although thankfully his father no longer had on his gas-mask. Chris was still wearing his short grey trousers, white shirt and blue pullover.

'You fell asleep, sissy,' said Chris. He was kneeling beside the blanket with his stick held over his knees.

'Hey,' reproached his father, clipping Chris lightly on the arm.

'Is that ... is that all?' Benton had a vague memory of a shot being fired.

'What's the matter, darling?' asked his mother.

'I'm not sure,' Benton replied, raising a hand to his aching head. 'I'm just not sure.'

'A touch of the sun?' his father wondered. 'You nearly missed your sponge cake.'

'Yes,' chided his mother, 'and it took nearly a month of coupons just to get the eggs.'

Benton looked down at the picnic food, arranged on the blanket beside the wicker basket in which it had been brought. It was meagre fare, of course, on account of the wartime rationing; but one thing he had always admired his mother for was the way she had tried to maintain a semblance of normality for her kids, even when times were hard. A look of puzzlement briefly clouded his features. Where was his older brother, George? Then he remembered: George had stayed at home that day to look after baby Charlotte. So ... this was not a full family outing. Maybe if his other two siblings had been there too, things would have turned out differently ... This train of thought was broken as he saw his father checking his watch and heard his mother asking:

'Everything all right?'

'I'll have to be making tracks soon,' came the regretful reply. 'Embarkation leave's nearly over.'

'So soon?' lamented his mother. 'Seems only like yesterday.'

'Don't go, Dad,' pleaded Chris. 'Please don't go. I hate it when you leave!'

'I'm a soldier, son,' his father reminded him. 'Duty calls. I have to go back.'

'Can I be a soldier, Father?' Benton asked, eagerly. 'A Sergeant, like you?'

'Of course, son. Maybe even better.'

'An officer?'

'Ah, well ...'

'Of course, Johnnie,' his mother chipped in, indulgently. 'If you want.'

'Well *I* don't!' countered Chris.

'Enough!' his father cautioned him.

'Well I *don't*. I don't want to die.'

'Christopher!' his mother scolded.

'It's stupid! War's stupid!' insisted Chris.

'I said *enough*!' shouted his father.

His mother laid a restraining hand on her husband's arm. 'Father, no. Please ...'

Reining in his temper with a visible effort, the soldier gently cuffed Chris around his fair-haired head.

Chris got to his feet and ran off in the direction of

a nearby stone archway. 'I'm off,' he called. 'Coming, Johnnie?'

Benton also rose from the picnic. 'Back soon,' he said, as his mother patted him affectionately on the arm. Then he chased after his brother.

It was six months later. Benton was back with his parents in the same spot, kneeling once again beside the picnic blanket. But things were different this time. His mother had on a plainer dress; his father lay stiffly on the grass, his posture awkward and his uniform jacket buttoned up to the neck; and, most significant of all, of course, there was no Chris with them ...

'Anybody want any more?' asked his mother, indicating the barely-touched food laid out on paper plates on the blanket.

'Not for me,' replied his father.

'That was great,' said Benton. 'Thanks, Mum.'

Noticing her husband checking his watch, his mother launched into a repeat of the previous year's conversation, asking him, 'Everything all right?'

'I'm fine,' he replied. 'I'll have to be making tracks soon. Embarkation leave's nearly over.'

'So soon,' she said, sadly. 'Seems only like yesterday.'

This time, it was Benton who objected, his agitation bringing out the native Lancastrian tones in his voice: 'Please don't go, Father. Don't go. You know I hate it when you leave!'

'I'm a soldier, son!' came the irritated reply. 'Duty calls. I have to go back.'

'But you'll die,' Benton insisted. 'You'll die out

there!'

Horrified, his mother tried to silence him: 'Johnnie!'

Benton, though, went on frantically: 'You'll be blown to pieces in a town in Normandy! They'll throw a grenade and you'll be blown into so many pieces that they won't find enough to give you a decent burial!'

'Johnnie, that's horrible!' protested his mother. 'Stop it! Please stop it, this minute!'

'But it's real!' Benton insisted. 'It's true! I've still got the letter!'

Reaching into the top pocket of his camouflage jacket, Benton pulled out a crumpled sheet of paper and brandished it at his father, who stared at it in wide-eyed alarm.

Suddenly reality shifted again, and Benton was actually there in Normandy, amidst the sound and fury of violent wartime action. A gas-masked British soldier, seeking cover in the ruins of a rough stone building, was cut down by a hail of machine-gun fire. Benton ran to his aid, pulling aside the gas-mask, but it was too late: the man was already dead, fresh blood staining his heavily-stubbled face. Arriving on the scene, Benton's father saw what had happened and gave a furious exclamation: 'Don't bloody gawp at him, man – move!' So saying, he abandoned the shelter of the ruins and set off in the direction from which the gunfire had come, determined to avenge his fallen comrade-in-arms. Benton shouted after him, trying to stop him, but to no avail, as instantly his senses were assailed by the blinding flash and thunderous roar of a grenade explosion. There was no way his father could have survived it.

When Benton's sight cleared, he found himself back at the picnic site, where his mother was sobbing over the official letter informing her of her husband's death in action.

'Don't worry, Mother,' he comforted her, the vision of the grenade explosion still vividly fresh in his mind. 'I'll look after you. I'll be just like Father, I will. I'll be just like him!' But he could barely hold back his own tears.

Back at the Land Rover, Willis's headache had grown worse rather than better, and he was now in a state of total confusion. He was powerless to protect himself as the man who had been stalking him emerged from the cover of the roadside undergrowth, ran up to him and felled him with a straight punch to the jaw.

In the still rational recesses of his mind, Benton was fully aware that the visions he was experiencing weren't real; that they were the product of some kind of psychic attack. But being aware of it and being able to do something about it were two different things. His grief over his father's death felt as painfully acute now as it had when he was a boy. He steeled himself to keep one thought clearly in mind: that he was on a UNIT mission and was meant to be returning to Willis at the Land Rover. He began retracing his path down the uneven stone steps of the overgrown gardens, casting occasional nervous glances backwards over his shoulder. Pausing to take a breath, he sensed rather than saw a man come up to stand behind him.

'Johnnie!' called the man, and Benton turned to find the gas-masked figure of his father, now laughing at him.

Benton cradled his aching head in hands. 'Go away, Father!' he pleaded. 'You don't exist. You're dead. You died years ago!'

In his mind's eye, Benton saw his father remove his gas-mask to reveal not the familiar features of his face but the horrible, leering skull of a corpse. Feeling his sanity slipping away, he redoubled his mental efforts to resist the psychic assault, crying out desperately: 'Go away!'

When he looked back again, he was relieved to find that, although he could still see his father's uniformed figure, the face had reverted to normal and the gas-mask had vanished.

'The grave's a fine and private place, Johnnie,' his father said. 'It's no disgrace to be dead. Besides, we were heroes.'

'Yes, but you don't understand, Father. You cannot exist. You're just a product of my imagination!'

'Imagination! You have no imagination, Johnnie! You never did!'

'I don't need imagination. Not in my job.'

'Oh, aye, your job. What rank are you now, Johnnie? Captain yet?'

'No!'

'What?'

Benton realised that he was being goaded, his insecurities exploited, but he couldn't resist rising to the bait. 'No!'

'Major?'

'No!'

'*Brigadier*, perhaps?'

'No. I'm a Warrant Officer, and that's good enough for me.'

'Had to be better than your old dad, eh, Johnnie?'

'I wanted to be *like* you, not better than you.'

'Your brother Chris, now. *He* was officer material.'

'Yes, well,' reflected Benton bitterly, 'you always liked him better than you liked me.'

'*He'd* have made a Captain.'

'He was always your favourite. He was always *given* what I had to *fight* for.'

'*He'd* have made Brigadier.'

'Yes, but *he* didn't want to, did he?' Benton retorted, squaring up to his father. '*He* didn't want to join the Army. *He* didn't want to be like you. *I* did! All I wanted was your approval, like you gave Chris!'

'So ... you *were* jealous of Chris.'

'He was my brother. I loved him.'

'You killed him, Johnnie,' goaded the voice.

'No, it was an accident.'

'You pushed him, Johnnie!'

'No, he fell, Father!'

'You pushed him, Johnnie. You killed my Christopher!'

'No, it was an accident. He fell!'

His father's voice was becoming harsh, grating, almost inhuman now: 'You killed him, Johnnie. You killed him!'

'Stop calling me Johnnie!' bellowed Benton. 'My name is *John*!'

This angry outburst momentarily broke the spell, and Benton was able to tear his eyes away from his father's phantom form. Instead, he saw again young Chris, still dressed as he had been before, but now with a soldier's steel helmet perched on his head, held in place by its leather chinstrap.

'Sissy!' taunted his brother.

As his father's laughter rang out once more and the air around him grew colder still, Benton sensed that the situation was coming to a head, and that his unseen attacker was about to launch a final, all-out assault on his sanity.

A bewildering, kaleidoscopic jumble of memories – brief, disjointed fragments of recollection – started flashing through his mind, as if images of everything he had experienced since arriving at Rivington Gardens were being sliced up and thrown back at him.

'It's our game, Johnnie,' jeered his father. 'We can call you anything we want to.'

'Sissy!' shouted Chris again.

'It's a game.' his father repeated. 'And it's not over yet.'

'Sissy!' came Chris's voice yet again.

'It was an accident, Chris, I swear!' insisted Benton.

'Time to run, Johnnie!' called Chris. 'I'm coming to get you!'

Benton knew full well that his attacker was using against him the feelings of guilt that he had never quite been able to shake off, even though he was sure in his heart that he had not been to blame for his brother's death. But, despite that, he ran, as he sensed Chris chasing after him and his father's mocking laughter ringing in his ears.

In no time at all they were back at the Tower. From the shadow of an archway, Benton watched as Chris raced up the flights of stone steps, ascending as quickly as his young legs would carry him, just as he had on that fateful day back in 1944. It all seemed so real; as if time had somehow been wound back and he himself was a young boy again, chasing his brother up those flights of steps, looking on as he let his stick – his pretend rifle – drop to the ground, climbing higher and higher still.

He remembered how Chris had called out to him: 'Johnnie! I can see you, Johnnie!'

Then he saw Chris balanced precariously on the narrow stone ledge just above him. Desperately he reached up, trying to grab hold of Chris's leg, to save him from falling, but he couldn't quite make it: all he was left with, grasped in his outstretched hand, was Chris's empty shoe, dislodged from his foot as he plunged to his death on the jagged rocks below.

Benton allowed himself a deep sigh of relief as he realised that his psychic attacker, far from getting the better of him, had inadvertently done him an incredible service: all those lingering feelings of guilt that he had harboured for so many years had now been finally dispelled. 'I *was* trying to save him,' he repeated triumphantly, certain now that he had not been mistaken. 'I *was*!'

At last, in his mind, Chris could truly rest in peace.

After a brief spell of disorientating dizziness, Benton found that he was kneeling back on the ground before the familiar piece of fallen masonry on which he and Chris had once chalked their initials. It seemed to him that he could still see a trace of those initials, now marked out not in chalk but in trickles of bright red blood. But despite this unsettling vision, he sensed that the danger had now passed: he had managed to weather and repel the psychic attack. His head was quickly clearing, and he wondered if everything he had experienced since he had last knelt in this spot had been purely illusory. He suspected it had. Before he could give the matter any further thought, though, his attention was caught by the distant sound of Willis's voice crying out in pain. Instantly he got to his feet and raced back through the gardens in the direction of the road.

As Willis struggled groggily to raise himself from where he had been poleaxed at the roadside, he saw that his assailant – a stocky, dark-haired man wearing a green canvas jacket and track-suit bottoms and holding a handgun – was reaching into the back of the Land Rover and setting down the gun so that he could take hold of the metal crate within. At that moment, though, Benton emerged from between the trees and pushed his rifle into the small of the would-be thief's back, issuing the terse instruction: 'Hold it.'

If Benton had expected a meek surrender, he was badly mistaken. Whirling around, the man grabbed hold of the rifle barrel and twisted it from Benton's grasp, then began laying into him with a series of heavy blows, slamming him into the side of the Land

Rover. Benton, though, fought back, returning his opponent's punches, kneeing and elbowing him in the midriff, then clouting him on the chin.

It was Benton who came out on top, leaving the younger man sprawled unconscious on the ground. Pausing only briefly to catch his breath, he ran across to Willis, who was gradually recovering.

'Willis, what happened?' he demanded.

'He came out the bushes, just after you'd gone, sir.'

'Okay. Come on.'

Benton was anxious not to linger here any longer. He was acutely conscious of the fact that, but for his decision to take an unauthorised detour and visit Chris's grave, this incident might never have happened. But, then again, had he been fully in his right mind when he had made that decision … ?

Willis rose gingerly to his feet and retrieved his rifle from where it had fallen on the ground, then ran over to join Benton at the Land Rover. Having stowed their weapons inside and lowered the tailgate, they both grabbed hold of their unconscious assailant and dumped him unceremoniously in the back of the vehicle, alongside the crate.

'Are you okay to drive?' Benton asked.

'Yes, sir,' Willis replied, relieved to realise that his headache had finally subsided.

'Then let's go.' So saying, Benton climbed into the back of the Land Rover, took up his rifle and sat with his foot firmly planted on the unconscious prisoner's back. Once they were well under way, he intended to bind the man hand and foot with a roll of gaffer tape he had spotted lying in one corner.

Willis meanwhile settled into the driver's seat,

fired up the engine and got the Land Rover moving again.

As Rivington Gardens receded into the distance behind them, Benton thought that he could still hear a faint echo of his father's voice, insisting: 'It *was* a game Johnnie. And it's over now ...'

But Benton wasn't fooled: he knew that it had been far from a game; and that in all probability it was not yet over. Now that his head was finally clear again, he was struck by a realisation that for some reason had previously escaped him – or perhaps more likely had been deliberately blocked from his mind – but now seemed blindingly obvious: it was the alien in the crate that had been responsible for the attack on his sanity, causing him to hallucinate just as it had his SAS comrades back in Iraq. Thankfully, like all UNIT operatives, he had received some training in how to resist hypnotism and other forms of mental control, so perhaps that had stood him in good stead. But be that as it may, he was puzzled: he had been certain that the creature was dead, so how could this have happened? Maybe he had been mistaken, and it had been merely injured, put out of action for a while, just as it must have been when its ship first landed in the Iraqi desert. Who knew how its alien physiology worked? Mercifully, there had been no hint of it causing any problems on the flight back to the UK; but perhaps it had been still recovering, biding its time until it regained at least a little of its strength. Of one thing Benton was certain: somehow the creature was still active, and still posed a potential threat. Grimly, he grasped his rifle more tightly, steeling himself for any further trouble that might lie ahead.

4
End Game

Northumberland, Monday 27 October 1990, Evening

There had been a change of plan. Travelling south on the M6 motorway, Benton had finally succeeded in contacting the Brigadier on the Land Rover's radio-telephone. His succinct account of his strange experiences at Rivington Gardens, and his conclusion that the 'shipment' was somehow still active, had been enough to convince Lethbridge-Stewart that it was now too dangerous for the crate to be brought to UNIT HQ. Instead, Private Willis had been ordered to divert northwards to the Cheviot Hills in Northumberland, to a facility called the Vault.

Willis, understandably, had never heard of the Vault, but Benton had been there several times before. It was the place to which most of the otherworldly artefacts captured or otherwise acquired during UNIT operations were ultimately taken for long-term scientific investigation and storage. That being the case, Benton reflected, the creature from the Iraqi site might well have ended up there anyway, after an initial examination at UNIT HQ; so this was really just a kind of short cut.

The sun was starting to set by the time Willis at last turned the Land Rover onto the approach road to the twin hills that housed the Vault. When the facility had been constructed, on Prime Minister Harold Wilson's instructions back in the 1960s, these hills had been essentially hollowed out, and inside each was constructed an eight-storey complex of offices, laboratories, storage units and living quarters. It was to the left-hand of the two hills that Benton directed Willis to drive, as he knew that this was where the camouflaged vehicle entrance was situated.

Word on the military grapevine was that the Vault was in the process of being transferred fully into UNIT's control, to be absorbed into its own Black Archive of especially sensitive alien material; but for the time being it was still administered, as it had been for some years, by C19, the MoD department that oversaw UNIT's British activities. Consequently, most of the basic security duties there were undertaken not by UNIT troops but by regular Army men who'd been given special clearance and placed on temporary secondment. It was one such officer, a Lieutenant Douglas Cavendish, who received Benton and Willis after they were cleared through the heavily-guarded vehicle entrance and Willis brought the Land Rover to rest in the parking bay.

Their arrival was expected, UNIT HQ having alerted the Vault to the situation, and four squaddies were immediately on hand to lift the crate out of the vehicle and carry it away into the bowels of the facility, while two others grabbed the securely-restrained prisoner, now conscious again but saying nothing, and dragged him off in a different direction. Willis meanwhile was stood down and, with considerable relief, hurried off to find the canteen.

Having exchanged a customary salute with Cavendish, Benton was led away to be debriefed.

Exactly how much time had passed since he and Willis had arrived at the Vault, Benton wasn't entirely sure, but it seemed like hours. He ran a hand over his tired eyes and leant back in his chair, stretching his legs out in front of him to try to relieve the stiffness in them. He was sat on one side of a table in a small, airless meeting room bathed in the harsh glare of a solitary ceiling strip-light, reminding him very much of the room in which he had received his initial mission briefing from the MI6 man Baker down in London, less than three weeks earlier. After they had left the parking bay, Lieutenant Cavendish had taken him up seven floors in a lift, ushered him along a maze of office-lined corridors and eventually shown him into this room. Then he had sat him down and proceeded to question him in forensic detail about everything that had happened in Iraq and everything he and Willis had experienced at Rivington Gardens, all the time making copious notes on a laptop. Now, though, Benton was alone in the room, Cavendish having been temporarily summoned away by a phone call. He was grateful to have these few moments to himself. Having to recount blow-by-blow the horrifying events of the past few days had taken a lot out of him. But that was not the only thing that had troubled him. Disconcertingly, Cavendish had seemed more intrigued than perturbed by what he was hearing and had taken a strange fascination in Benton's professionally precise description of the alien creature and its apparent demise. The Lieutenant had a supercilious manner that did not sit well with Benton and had been clearly unconvinced by his warning that the creature could still pose a real danger.

As Benton sat mulling all this over, the strip-light overhead started flickering slightly. Re-entering the room, Cavendish noticed it too and glanced up briefly, but made no comment as the flickering quickly stopped.

'So,' said Cavendish, resuming his seat on the opposite side of the table to Benton, 'it seems our friends at UNIT HQ have managed to identify the man who attacked you and your driver. His name's Barrie O'Keefe. They've been taking an interest in him for quite a while, as it happens. Apparently, he's one of a small network of international agents working undercover for a stinkingly rich but decidedly dodgy American entrepreneur named van Statten, who's secretly – or so he thinks – trying to assemble his own private collection of recovered alien artefacts.'

'Seriously?' Benton was astounded. 'That's madness!'

'You think so?' mused Cavendish. 'It's not all that different from what we're doing here, is it?'

'But alien tech isn't something for civilians to be messing about with. It can be incredibly dangerous!'

'You've been serving in UNIT since almost the start,' noted Cavendish, 'and must have seen a lot of extraordinary stuff in your time. Have you never been tempted to take home a few … souvenirs?'

Benton didn't know quite what to say. Was the

man joking, or trying to catch him out in some way? 'No, sir,' was all the reply he could manage.

'Well, anyway,' Cavendish went on, 'O'Keefe's being packed off to the Glasshouse now for interrogation. Actually, I gather your friend Spadger Hughes is on his way there too, to recuperate from his injury and be debriefed. Though I doubt they'll be bumping into each other.'

The Glasshouse, Benton knew, was a C19-funded private medical facility near Evesham in Worcestershire. It was where people who'd had 'close encounters' were generally taken to be checked over and, if necessary, treated by doctors, interviewed by UNIT officers, and in some rare cases – such as where collaboration with would-be alien invaders was either proved or suspected – detained for security reasons. Rumour had it that a few of those who ended up there were never seen again.

'Does that mean–?' Benton began, but broke off as the ceiling light started flickering again and then went out altogether, plunging the room into sudden darkness.

'Damn!' exclaimed Cavendish. 'The bulb must have blown. Sorry about this. I'll have someone call maintenance and get it fixed.'

Benton heard the Lieutenant scrape his chair back, feel his way cautiously along the wall and pull open the door. But rather than the room being instantly flooded with bright light from the corridor beyond, only the dull red glow of emergency lighting seeped in through the open doorway.

'That's strange,' muttered Cavendish, evidently puzzled. 'We've got our own generators here, so we shouldn't be having a power cut.'

Suddenly the air was split by the shrill, repetitive blasts of a warning klaxon.

'What the hell's going on?' cursed Cavendish.

It took Benton only a moment to work it out. 'It's that alien,' he said. 'I told you, it can draw energy from its surroundings to revive itself and attack people. It must be feeding off the electricity from your generators.'

'I'm sure we've got security measures in place to stop that kind of thing happening,' said Cavendish; but his voice betrayed considerable doubt. All trace of his earlier complacent manner had now vanished, and he seemed, Benton thought, rather like a deer caught in headlights.

'Sir,' prompted Benton gently, 'we ought to check out what's happening.'

At this, the younger man seemed to pull himself together. 'Of course, you're right, Mr Benton. Follow me.'

So saying, he led Benton rapidly back through the dimly-lit corridors, reversing the route they had taken earlier. When they reached the lift, though, they found that it was out of action: another casualty of the power drain.

'We'll have to use the stairs,' stated Cavendish. 'The crate with the alien in will have been taken to Laboratory 1 on the first floor for an initial investigation. Not the cleverest of moves, in retrospect.'

'What do you mean?' asked Benton.

'The generators are just below that, in the service area near the parking bay,' admitted Cavendish ruefully.

'Maybe we could get down there and disable

them – cut off the energy flow?' suggested Benton. 'Rather than trying to tackle the creature directly?'

'That's not a bad idea,' agreed Cavendish, tacitly accepting now that the creature must be at the root of the trouble. 'Come on.'

With that, he pushed open a door in a narrow recess to one side of the lift and started bounding down the bare concrete staircase beyond. With a sigh, Benton got his stiff legs into motion and hurried after him.

As they were making their way down the stairs, floor by floor, the warning klaxon suddenly cut out. Benton was relieved; it had been starting to give him a headache. Or perhaps, he realised, it was alien's slowly growing mental influence that was causing the headache. He was wise to the signs now, and noted with grim satisfaction that the air temperature in the stairwell had also fallen significantly. This time, he told himself, he would not succumb so easily to any psychic attack.

When they reached the third-floor landing, they almost ran into three squaddies who were milling about there, uncertain what to do.

'You men, follow me,' ordered Cavendish. 'We need to get down to the ground floor and try to put the generators out of action.'

The three men exchanged brief looks of puzzlement but obeyed unquestioningly, falling into line behind Cavendish and Benton as they continued their rapid descent.

On reaching the first-floor landing they all paused briefly, alarmed by a cacophony of shrieks and wails that they could hear coming from beyond the connecting door to the corridor. One of the squaddies, a glazed expression on his face, made to open the door and go through, but Cavendish grabbed hold of his arm and held him back.

'We can't … we can't help them like that,' muttered Cavendish, talking almost as if to himself. He held his hands to his temples, obviously trying to marshal his thoughts.

Benton cast a worried look at the young officer, wondering how much resilience he might have to the full-on mental assault that seemed certain to come. Being a regular Army man, not a UNIT agent, he would have received no training in resistance techniques. To his relief, though, he saw that Cavendish had quickly regained his composure and was now heading off again down the final flight of stairs to the ground floor. Benton went after him, leaving the three squaddies to bring up the rear.

Reaching the foot of the staircase, they pushed their way through the last connecting door and into the lift lobby beyond. To their right was another door, which Benton recalled coming through earlier on, when being brought in from the parking bay; but this time Cavendish led the small party in the opposite direction, along a passageway that eventually opened out into a cavernous, concrete-floored service area. At the far end, Benton saw a pair of sturdy metal shutters marked with hazard warning decals and a large red sign reading 'Beware – Danger of Electrocution'. Cavendish indicated the shutters, which were standing slightly open.

'That's the generator room,' he muttered. 'But it's odd: those shutters should be kept fully closed and secured.'

Cautiously, the five men started to advance across

the floor, Cavendish and Benton taking the lead. Even the dull red emergency lighting was faltering here, rapidly rising and falling in intensity, creating a hellish strobe-like effect. Suddenly one of the three squaddies cried out in anguish.

'Sir ... Sorry, sir ... I don't think I can go on ...'

Looking back, Benton saw that the man was holding his head in his hands and shaking violently.

'Get a grip, Private!' hissed Cavendish, waving him forward.

This, though, was to no avail, as the man seemed rooted to the spot. Moments later, another of the squaddies fell to his knees, wailing softly. Cavendish turned to the third.

'What about you, Henderson? Are you still with us?'

'My head's hurting like buggery, sir,' Henderson replied, grimacing, 'but I think I'm okay.'

'Good man,' nodded Cavendish. 'Come on then.'

They set off again toward the generator room and quickly covered the remaining distance. Motioning Henderson to help him, Benton was about to pull the shutters wider apart when suddenly the heavy metal panels were flung open from within and they found themselves confronted by five menacing figures crouched in the semi-darkness beyond. Two of the five were maintenance men wearing grimy boiler suits, while the other three were regular soldiers: two male and one female. The most striking thing about them, though, was the hideous contorted expressions on their faces. Snarling viciously and with spittle running down their chins, they looked like wild animals, almost as if they had been physically transformed. Benton had a sudden vivid memory of how, back at the dawn of the 1970s, when he was newly promoted to Sergeant, he had witnessed some of his men being regressed to slavering primordial creatures at the ill-fated Project Inferno.

'Back!' he shouted, as the five bestial figures began moving threateningly forward, their hands outstretched before them like claws.

'What's the hell's going on, sir?' shrieked Henderson, completely bewildered.

'Their minds are being affected by a captured alien on the level above,' explained Benton succinctly. 'I think it's using them to protect the generators, to make sure its power supply can't be cut off.'

By this point, they had been forced back across the floor to the place where they had left the other two squaddies, who had now both collapsed to the concrete and were rolling around in agony, obviously incapable of offering any assistance. Drawing his handgun from its holster, Cavendish fired a warning shot over the heads of the five approaching figures, but this did nothing to deter their remorseless progress.

'What now?' asked Cavendish, a note of panic creeping into his voice. 'I doubt very much that we can overpower them, and there's no way I'm actually going to shoot our own people.'

Peering at the menacing figures more closely, Benton suddenly realised that he recognised the three soldiers: they had been stationed at the vehicle entrance when he and Willis had first arrived at the Vault, and had given their papers the once-over before clearing them for admittance and raising the security barrier. Presumably, under the alien's influence, they must have abandoned their posts.

'Back to the vehicle entrance,' he told Cavendish. 'There must be some more weapons there, in the guard room. We'll just have to try tackling the creature directly after all.'

'Okay, that sounds like a plan,' agreed Cavendish, returning his handgun to its holster. 'Let's go.'

Reluctantly leaving their two stricken comrades where they had fallen, Cavendish, Benton and Henderson began retreating more rapidly, still keeping their eyes apprehensively fixed on the danger behind them. They had almost reached the passageway leading to the lift lobby when, as if at a silent signal, the five stalking figures suddenly leapt forward and pounced on them, shrieking and howling like banshees. In their derangement, they seemed possessed of almost superhuman strength, frenziedly punching, kicking, scratching, even biting.

It was the two boiler-suited maintenance men who set upon Benton; but although they were well-built, they were obviously unused to physical combat, and he found that he could parry their clumsy, uncoordinated blows more easily than he had expected. He almost surprised himself with his own strength as, after a brief skirmish, he managed to knock them both unconscious.

Quickly he ran to the aid of Henderson, who was trying with increasing desperation to free himself from a vice-like choke-hold in which one of the male soldiers had caught him. Having lost precious seconds trying without success to prise the soldier's fingers from around Henderson's throat, Benton resorted to felling the man with a powerful two-fisted blow to the back of his neck. Henderson, though, also slumped to the floor, either unconscious or dead; Benton had no time to stop and find out, as Cavendish had meanwhile been forced to his knees and was trying as best as he could to fend off the brutal assault being mounted on him by the other two crazed soldiers.

Benton launched himself into the fray, but almost at once began to regret it, thinking that he had perhaps bitten off more than he could chew. The two attackers were unleashing a furious barrage of punches and kicks on him and Cavendish, gradually beating them down through sheer brute force. Benton had hoped that the female soldier might be physically weaker than her male counterparts, but there was no sign of that being the case. As he sank to the floor, he tried to grab hold of her wrists to restrain her, but she easily shook off his grip and slashed her sharp fingernails viciously down his cheek, drawing blood. His already depleted reserves of strength were rapidly diminishing, and he was starting to fear that he and Cavendish were done for, when suddenly he saw a flash of red movement above him, accompanied by two loud clunking noises. Instantly the two attackers ceased their onslaught and fell unconscious to the floor. Looking up, Benton was amazed to see the familiar figure of Private Willis standing there, wielding a bulky metal fire-extinguisher like a club.

'Good work, Private!' he exclaimed. 'But what are you doing here?'

'I was on my way back to my Land Rover, sir, when the power went out and I got stuck in the lift. I'd just managed to force the doors open when I heard a right old commotion coming from in here and decided I'd better investigate.'

'I'm very glad you did, Willis. I don't think we could have held out much longer.'

'It's like what happened at Rivington Gardens, isn't it, sir? I can feel the same kind of headache coming on, and I'm having trouble focusing.'

Benton nodded in confirmation. 'You're right. But there's no time to explain now. Help me with the Lieutenant.'

So saying, Benton rose from the floor and, with Willis's assistance, hauled the groggy Cavendish back to his feet.

'Do you need to rest for a bit, sir?' he asked him.

'I'll be all right,' snapped Cavendish, with a mixture of annoyance and embarrassment. 'Let's get to that guard room.' So saying, he staggered off down the exit passageway.

Benton hesitated momentarily, thinking that he really ought to check on Henderson, but then reluctantly acknowledged that there were higher priorities right now. He sped off after Cavendish, motioning Willis to follow.

The three men passed quickly through the lift lobby – where, thanks to Willis's handiwork, the lift doors were now standing partly open, revealing that it had come to a halt a couple of feet short of the floor – then went on through into the parking bay and across to the vehicle entrance.

As Benton had hoped, the guard room adjacent to the security barrier had been left deserted, its door standing ajar. He followed Cavendish inside, with Willis hot on his heels.

'Over here,' instructed Cavendish.

Reaching inside the neck of his combat jacket, the

Lieutenant pulled out a key-card attached to a lanyard and swiped it down a reader positioned on the far wall of the room alongside a heavily-reinforced door. The reader emitted a shrill beep in response, then the door slid slowly open. Benton gave a low whistle as inside was revealed a cabinet packed with a small arsenal of various types of weapons, all neatly arrayed in metal racks.

Cavendish reached into the cabinet, grabbed a pair of handguns and shoved them into his belt alongside the one he already had in his holster. Then he stuffed his pockets full of grenades. Finally he took hold of a powerful-looking machine-gun. Benton also reached into the cabinet and removed two handguns; one of these he stashed in his own belt, the other he passed to the increasingly troubled-looking Willis. However, after a brief contemplation of the remaining weapons, he decided against following Cavendish's example and taking any more. It had been some years since he had last had a practice session on a firing range, and he strongly suspected a machine-gun would be more of an encumbrance to him than a help.

'Okay, let's do this,' said Cavendish, and headed back out of the room. Willis made to follow him, but staggered to one side and collided with the doorpost. Benton placed a restraining hand on his shoulder.

'Willis, you'd better stay here,' he told him. Seeing that the man was about to object, he added quickly, 'I want you to get on the blower to UNIT HQ and let them know what's happening. We might well need outside help.'

Willis raised a hand to his temple and shook his head in confusion. 'But I don't really know what *is* happening, sir,' he protested.

'Just tell them it's an emergency!' Benton insisted; and without further delay he set off at a run toward the lift lobby.

Benton kept close behind Cavendish as they ascended the concrete staircase to the first floor. They were moving more carefully now, peering into the red gloom ahead of them, staying alert for any fresh danger that might arise. Benton was acutely aware that the alien creature must be growing in strength all the time. His head was throbbing painfully now, and the temperature had fallen so low that, when he exhaled, his breath misted the air in front of him. He could see that Cavendish was suffering too: he was having to hold on to the metal handrail for support; his face was contorted in a frightful grimace; and, despite the cold, sweat was trickling down his forehead. Regardless, Benton reflected, the younger man must have some natural mental resilience: even though he lacked the benefit of Benton's own prior experience of the creature's insidious psychic influence, he still had yet to succumb. How much longer that would continue to be the case, though, remained to be seen.

They reached the first-floor landing without incident and Cavendish cautiously led the way through the connecting door and into the corridor beyond. The horrible shrieks and wails they had heard filtering through from here earlier on had now ceased; but the silence was ominous rather than reassuring. Slowly the two men made their way down the corridor. In the subdued lighting, Benton could just distinguish that although the right-hand wall was featureless, the left-hand one had inset at regular intervals along its length a row of bulky metal doors with signs indicating that they gave on to a series of sequentially-numbered storage areas. They had just crept past the third of these doors when the fourth was flung violently outwards from within, sheared from its hinges, and there emerged into the corridor ahead of them a grotesque alien creature, humanoid in form but a mottled orange in colour, with a large domed head and sucker-like protrusions covering its entire body.

'What the hell is that?' yelled Cavendish, frozen in his tracks.

Benton wasted no time in replying but instead drew his handgun from his belt, flipped off the safety catch and started pumping bullets into the creature as it strode rapidly toward them. After a moment's panicked hesitation, Cavendish levelled his machine-gun and also unleashed a hail of bullets. Under their combined firepower the creature really stood no chance; letting out an unearthly screech, it fell prostrate to the floor, its body almost ripped to shreds.

Visibly shaken, Cavendish went over and surveyed the blood-spattered remains, some parts of which were still twitching feebly. 'I don't understand,' he muttered. 'There shouldn't be any live aliens in this zone. It's for preserving dead specimens in cold storage.'

'I'm not sure it really was alive,' said Benton. 'I think our green friend from Iraq was probably just using it as a weapon against us.'

'You mean it has the power to reanimate?' asked

Cavendish, a feverish glint in his eyes.

'I doubt it. I think it was just controlling this poor devil's body like a puppet.'

Any further debate was forestalled as suddenly they heard a low, anguished moaning sound coming from around a junction leading off to the right at the far end of the corridor. Benton hurried forward but stopped just before reaching the corner as he realised that Cavendish was no longer with him. Looking back, he saw that the Lieutenant had got barely any farther than the wrecked storage area door: he was now leaning against the wall, doubled over in pain, his head in his hands. Benton faltered briefly, in two minds what to do, but then decided to leave Cavendish where he was for the time being and go on ahead.

Rounding the corner, he found himself in yet another corridor. This one, though, was not deserted: even in the dim emergency lighting he could make out the shadowy forms of several men and women slumped here and there along the floor. A couple of them were uniformed soldiers, the rest civilians, but all were evidently in a state of great distress. Quickly Benton crossed to the nearest of the stricken men, a middle-aged civilian wearing spectacles and the characteristic white lab coat of a scientist. It was he who was responsible for the low moaning they had heard from the adjoining corridor.

At Benton's approach, the man stirred a little and peered groggily up at him. 'Is that you, Mother?' he asked, his voice little more than a whisper.

Benton shook him urgently by the shoulder. 'Snap out of it, man!'

'I knew it was you, Mother,' the man replied, a

smile spreading slowly across his face.

In other circumstances, Benton had to admit, he might have found this distinctly comical; but that certainly wasn't the case now. 'Look,' he insisted, 'I'm not your Mother. That's just a trick, an illusion. You can fight it, resist it!'

'Resist it …?' the man echoed.

'That's right! Now, I want you to listen to me. I brought an alien back from Iraq. In a metal crate marked with radiation symbols. It was taken to …' Benton struggled to remember what Cavendish had said …'Laboratory 1, I think, to be examined. I need to know where that is!'

The scientist shook his head as if to try to clear it. 'I … I'm not sure …'

'Think, man, think!' Benton insisted. 'This is vital!'

Benton's headache was becoming almost unbearable now, and he wasn't sure how much longer he could continue to hold out against the alien's persistent probing of his mental defences. To his frustration, though, the scientist said nothing more, but simply fell back to the floor, plainly exhausted.

With a sigh, Benton was about to move on down the corridor and try talking to the next of the afflicted scientists when suddenly he felt someone grab hold of his arm from behind. He whirled around, bracing himself for another fight, but to his astonishment saw that it was Cavendish who had held him back, having obviously caught up with him unheard. A quick glance was all Benton needed to realise that the Lieutenant was in a bad way. He was twitching uncontrollably, his uniform was disarrayed and he had a wild-eyed expression on his face. Somehow, though, it seemed he was still just managing to cling on to his sanity.

'There's no need to ask these people,' Cavendish told him, his voice now reduced to a tortured rasp. 'I know the way. You just need to go down to the end of this corridor, turn right, down to the end of the next corridor, and the entrance to Laboratory 1 is on your right-hand side. Like I said before, it's directly above where the generators are. Have you got that?'

'I think so,' said Benton, 'but if not, you can just show me, can't you.'

Cavendish shook his head emphatically. 'I … I nearly attacked you just now,' he admitted, letting the machine-gun slip from his grasp and fall to the floor. 'That *thing* is inside my head. I can feel it. I can't be trusted anymore. You'll have to go on without me.'

This time it was Benton's turn to shake his head. 'No way,' he retorted. 'You're coming with me. I can't do this alone.'

Already feeling pangs of guilt at having left Henderson and the other squaddies to their fate in the service area, Benton had no intention of abandoning Cavendish as well. Besides which, he really didn't fancy the prospect of having to face the alien on his own, and wasn't even sure he could make it that far himself. Surely, he reasoned, two of them must stand more chance than one?

To his relief, Cavendish seemed disinclined to argue the point: with a resigned shrug, he lurched off in the direction he had indicated. Benton fell into step beside him, now and again reaching out to steady him as he seemed about to stumble and fall, and all the time keeping a wary eye on him. When they reached the final corridor leading to the laboratory, they saw at once that about a dozen more scientists, soldiers and Vault staff members were collapsed on the floor there, some of them in open doorways leading to side-rooms from which they'd obviously been in the process of emerging, perhaps in a vain attempt to evacuate the area when the klaxon sounded. They were all writhing around, clawing at the air and raving to themselves, as if each was tormented by the presence of something or someone that only he or she could see. Benton shuddered at the sight. It was like a scene out of a horror movie.

Slowly Benton and Cavendish made their way down the corridor. As they passed by, some of the pitiful, demented figures reached up to grasp and pull at their clothing – though whether this was in an attempt to impede their progress or simply in a desperate appeal for help, they couldn't be sure. One woman, dressed in the sharp business suit of an office administrator, even struggled to her feet and started to grapple with them, yelling incoherently; but they were able to brush her aside without much difficulty.

Having run this harrowing gauntlet, made all the more nightmarish by the dull, blood-red emergency lighting, they finally reached a clearer stretch of corridor, and Benton saw that there was a pair of double doors marked 'Laboratory 1' standing closed on the right-hand side up ahead, just as Cavendish had said there would be. Before they could advance any further, though, the Lieutenant dropped to his knees and let out a long, keening wail. Benton made to go to his aid, but a sudden wave of nausea pulled him up short. He shook his head, trying to clear it, but this served only to make the dizziness worse; and, still plagued by the incessant throb, throb, throb of his headache, he felt on the verge of passing out.

A sense of despair and frustration swept over him. Had he really come through all this just to fall at the final hurdle? But then, as had happened so often in the past, his UNIT training kicked in from his subconscious and gave him renewed hope. A basic resistance-to-psychic-attack technique, first told to him by a friend many years earlier, came back to him now, and he seized on it gratefully.

'Cavendish, think!' he shouted. 'What are three sevens?'

The Lieutenant looked up at him, bleary eyed and with a bemused expression on his face.

'What ...?'

'Three sevens!' insisted Benton.

'Twenty-one,' replied Cavendish automatically.

'That's it!' said Benton. 'Concentrate on the numbers. Twenty-one times five!'

'One hundred and five.'

'Minus twenty-seven!'

'Er ... seventy-eight.'

As Benton had hoped, the mental effort of working out these simple sums gave Cavendish something to focus on, weakening the alien's influence over him, and he visibly rallied. To his relief, Benton found that coming up with the sums also helped to clear his own mind. He hauled Cavendish back to his feet and almost dragged him down the remaining few feet of the corridor, all the time calling out further sums. He wasn't even certain that the rasped answers Cavendish was giving were correct – his mental arithmetic wasn't really up to it, particularly in this high-stress situation – but he knew that wasn't the point: as long as he continued to set the sums, and Cavendish continued to give the answers, their minds were occupied, forming an effective obstacle to the alien's interference.

They had now reached the set of double doors leading to Laboratory 1. The top half of each was indented with a large circular window, but when Benton tried to peer through to find out what was going on inside, he found that the glass was heavily frosted, giving no clear view of the interior.

'I guess we'll just have to see what we find once we're inside,' he muttered. But when he tried to push the doors open, he found that they wouldn't budge; they were obviously sealed.

On seeing this, Cavendish, who had been hanging back a little, swaying uncertainly from side to side, was prompted into action. Pushing himself forward, he produced from around his neck the same key-card he had used earlier in the guard room and swiped it down a reader that Benton hadn't spotted before, affixed to the wall just to the left of the doors.

Feeling even more thankful now that he had coaxed the Lieutenant into accompanying him on this final stretch of the tortuous route that had brought them to Laboratory 1, Benton waited apprehensively, bracing himself for action, as the reader beeped and the doors swung slowly open.

Moving cautiously forward into the laboratory, Benton was momentarily dazzled by the harsh green light that met his eyes, in stark contrast to the muted redness of the emergency lighting outside. When his vision started to clear, he dimly registered that several more lab-coated scientists were slumped unconscious over desks and instrument panels around the edges of the room; but his attention was inexorably drawn to what was happening in the centre. Lying on a work-bench, its lid thrown wide open, was the metal crate in which he and Spadger had brought the alien back from Iraq, while above it, hovering upright in mid-air, was the ghastly figure of the alien itself. Was it his imagination, Benton wondered, or had the creature actually grown in size since he had first encountered it? It looked about half as big again now, and it was difficult to see how it could ever have fitted inside the crate.

It was the alien that was the source of the intense green glow that bathed the area. There were small, lightning-like flashes of energy radiating outwards from its body, forming a sphere of light around it; an effect that put Benton incongruously in mind of a plasma-globe table-lamp his dear old aunt had once given him as a Christmas present. As he studied the alien more closely, he saw that there was a gaping hole in the centre of its chest where he had shot it back at the Iraqi dig site. Viscous dark-green liquid was slowly seeping from the jagged edges of the hole and trickling down its body to congeal in a small pool on the work-bench below. The creature, though, showed no signs of being troubled by this wound. In fact, it seemed stronger than ever, due no doubt to the copious amounts of power it was drawing from the Vault's generators. The injury it had previously had to its right-hand side appeared largely healed now; and Benton was disconcerted to see that its four tiny eyes were firmly fixed on him in a malevolent glare.

Suddenly a burst of gunshots rang out, and Benton looked round to see that Cavendish had entered the laboratory behind him and was aiming one of his handguns unsteadily in the alien's direction. Whether or not any of the bullets had struck their intended target, Benton couldn't be sure; but if they had, it was without any obvious effect. The creature slowly raised its left hand until it was pointing directly at Cavendish, then hurled a bolt of fiery green energy from its fingertips, striking him squarely in the head and sending him flying backwards to land with a thud against the laboratory wall. The Lieutenant made a brief attempt to struggle back to his feet but couldn't manage it; with a groan of pain, he flopped back against the wall, a dazed expression on his face, and let the handgun slip from his grasp.

Benton quickly returned his attention to the alien, but a sudden spike of excruciating pain pierced through his head and brought stars to his eyes, and he realised he was again close to blacking out. He tried desperately to focus, but the scene before him seemed to shift and blur, and in the centre of the room, where previously the alien had been, he now saw once more the familiar figure of his father, kitted out in his wartime uniform and gas-mask.

'So, you wanted to be a soldier, Johnnie,' came his father's scornful voice. 'Look where it's got you now! You're useless! Pathetic!'

'Father, go away, please,' pleaded Benton. 'You're not real! You were killed in action!'

'Now, now, Johnnie, don't start all that again,'

chided the phantom figure, drifting slowly forward to confront him. 'Chris would have known how to handle this, but let's face it, you've failed. Failed! And now you're dead!'

'No, Father! It's not me who's dead, it's you! You were ... you were ... blown to pieces ... in Normandy ... by a ... by a ... grenade!'

Suddenly it struck Benton that, just as the alien had inadvertently gifted him a cathartic epiphany back in Rivington Gardens, now it had unconsciously shown him a possible way out of this seemingly hopeless situation. Gathering the last vestiges of his strength, he ran across to where Cavendish was lying propped against the wall, rummaged in his jacket pockets and found one of the grenades he had stashed there earlier in the guard room. Then, pulling the pin, he lobbed the grenade into the centre of the room, where he knew deep down that it would find not his father but the hideous glowing form of the alien.

He just had time to grab Cavendish and pull him underneath a nearby table for cover before the grenade detonated with an almighty bang that reverberated around the walls and set his ears ringing. Instantly the green glow was extinguished, leaving the room in semi-darkness; but thankfully only a few seconds later the main ceiling lights flickered back on, filling the place with stark white illumination. Evidently the power drain was now ended.

When the dust had settled a little, Benton emerged from under the table and looked around, blinking as his eyes adjusted to the sudden brightness. He was relieved to have survived the explosion, but not altogether surprised: he remembered how, back in Iraq, the alien had managed to contain much of the energy of a grenade blast. Crucially, though, enough of the energy had still escaped for a luckless Iraqi guard to be blown to smithereens; and, as Benton crossed to the centre of the room, his headache at last weakening, he saw to his satisfaction that the alien itself had now met the same fate. Its body had been literally torn apart by the explosion, and assorted pieces of it were left lying scattered across the crate, the work-bench and the surrounding floor area, amidst swathes of the dark-green gunk that seemed to serve as its blood. This time, clearly, there was not the slightest danger of it making an unexpected recovery.

Benton allowed himself a grim smile of triumph as he realised that, finally, the crisis was over.

5
Aftermath

Northumberland, Tuesday 28 October 1990, Mid-Morning

Just before midnight, a squad of heavily-armed UNIT troops had landed at the Vault by military helicopter, responding to the panicked emergency call Willis had put in to their HQ in London. They had reacted with a mixture of relief and irritation to find that, by the time they got there, the action was all over and their presence was no longer really needed. Having helped to round up the wounded and ensure that they were receiving appropriate care and attention, while the mercifully few who were beyond help were carried off to a makeshift morgue, they had departed almost as quickly as they had arrived.

Staff who were based in the other of the Vault's twin hills, where most of the living quarters were situated, had scarcely felt the alien's influence, and a contingent of them had been summoned across the divide to support and stand in for the more badly afflicted of their colleagues, few of whom were in a fit state to work. Transportation was already being arranged for several small groups to be taken off to the Glasshouse for psychiatric evaluation, and Benton suspected that some would require long-term counselling.

In Laboratory 1, meanwhile, a major clean-up operation was under way. The worst of the blast damage was being patched up until proper repairs could be effected, and what was left of the alien's body had been carefully separated out, packed into a stack of plastic sample boxes, labelled up and taken away for storage pending a thorough examination. The dead alien that Benton and Cavendish had riddled with bullets in the corridor nearby had likewise been returned to storage, in a considerably worse state than when it had emerged.

Having managed to catch a few hours' fitful sleep in one of the on-site dormitories, Benton was now being escorted back to the parking bay by Cavendish. He had no idea what the alien's long-term intentions might have been – perhaps it had really had no plan at all, and had been acting purely on instinct, like an animal – but he wasn't concerned about that; he was just relieved that it was finally dead and could no longer pose a threat.

Outwardly at least, Cavendish seemed remarkably unaffected by his ordeal, and as they left the lift lobby and went through into the parking bay he was making bland small talk about the detailed report he would later have to write on the extraordinary incident. 'This kind of thing must be all in a day's work for you, I suppose,' he mused.

'Not exactly, sir,' replied Benton, with a wry smile. 'If every day was like this, it'd be too much excitement for me.'

'Personally, I could do with a bit more of that excitement,' said Cavendish. 'In fact, this has made up my mind: when I get back to my own regiment,

I'm going to put in a formal request for a permanent transfer to UNIT.'

Benton gave the Lieutenant an appraising look. He had certainly acquitted himself well during the emergency, particularly given his obvious inexperience and lack of training for such situations, but was he honestly UNIT material? Now that things were getting back to normal, the young officer's strange air of naïvely complacent superiority seemed to be resurfacing too. Was that really the right temperament for the job? Thankfully, Benton reflected, these things would be for others to decide, not him. 'I wish you luck, sir,' was all he offered in reply.

They had by now reached the Land Rover, where they found Private Willis waiting at the wheel, still little the wiser about what had really being going on over the last few hours. Having exchanged a parting salute with Cavendish, Benton crossed to the opposite side of the vehicle and climbed into the passenger seat. Then Willis started the engine, drove over to the guard post and, after a brief wait while the security barrier was raised, headed off down the approach road.

As the Vault receded into the distance behind them and they resumed their much-delayed journey down to UNIT HQ in London, Benton couldn't help but wonder what his next assignment would be. Whatever it was, he hoped to goodness it would be less stressful than the one he had just completed!

Author's Note

Written by Andy Lane and Helen Stirling and produced and directed by Reeltime Pictures' Keith Barnfather, the original *Wartime* video drama holds a special place in *Doctor Who* history. Released in 1988, just before the hiatus now commonly referred to by fans as the 'wilderness years', it was the very first independently-produced spin-off from the venerable BBC show. More ambitious examples have followed since – including from Reeltime Pictures themselves the feature-length *Downtime* – but *Wartime* was the trailblazer that arguably made all of those others possible. It is also a production for which I've always had a great deal of admiration and affection. It makes incredibly effective use of its very limited budget and resources, and to my mind still stands up well even today, giving the popular *Doctor Who* semi-regular John Benton, played by John Levene, the exciting solo adventure that the parent show was never able to afford him. Bearing all this in mind, I was very pleased and honoured to be entrusted with the responsibility of novelising the video for Telos Publishing, the company I co-own and run with David J Howe. This was also, though, a task that presented me with significant challenges.

One of those challenges arose from the simple fact that the *Wartime* video runs for barely half-an-hour – about the same duration as a single weekly episode of classic-era *Doctor Who* – and consists mainly of subjective, dream-like sequences with relatively sparse dialogue. Had I stuck to novelising only the scripted material from the video itself, the end product would probably have been more akin to a pamphlet than a book. Thus came about the idea of expanding the story into three main sections of roughly equal word-count, with the video material forming the second section and becoming, as it were, the filling in a narrative sandwich. For inspiration for the opening and closing sections, I turned to the video's original scriptwriters, Andy Lane and Helen Stirling, both of whom were supportive and enthusiastic. Andy kindly wrote for me a detailed storyline suggesting how *Wartime* might be expanded into a larger-scale adventure, and although in the end I chose to depart from its specifics and develop the story in a slightly different way, the basic ideas he came up with – having the first section set mainly in Iraq during the Gulf War, with an alien artefact being dug up from the desert, and the last section set mainly in a military establishment back in the UK, with the alien influence wreaking havoc – remain at the heart of those sections of the finished text. Other suggestions came from Keith Barnfather, who was particularly keen that the expanded story should involve, as a young man, the Douglas Cavendish character originally created by Marc Platt for *Downtime* and subsequently featured in another Reeltime Pictures production, the David J Howe-scripted *Dæmos Rising*. The book is still not a long one – more novella length than novel – but I make no apologies for that. To have expanded the framing story any further would have risked the original video material becoming merely a minor incident within a much more elaborate plot, and would I feel have departed too far from the essential concept of a novelisation.

The other challenge I faced in tackling this task had more to do with my own experience as an author than with the source material itself. When I first started writing in earnest in the late 1970s, I vaguely assumed that I would divide my efforts roughly equally between non-fiction and fiction. As things transpired, though, I soon became essentially pigeonholed as a non-fiction specialist. I have no complaints about that – I love writing non-fiction – but it does mean that, over the years, I have taken on relatively few fiction projects. There have of course been exceptions: I remain especially proud of the fact that, with Mark Stammers, I initiated and was one of the original editors on Virgin Publishing's *Decalog* books, the very first officially-licensed *Doctor Who* short story collections; and since then I have edited many novels and short stories penned by other authors for Telos Publishing. The fact was, though, that when I started work on this novelisation of *Wartime*, it had been some years since I had last written fiction for publication (as opposed to for my own amusement), and I was concerned that I might be somewhat rusty. Thankfully, as things turned out, I soon got back into the swing of fiction writing; and, if I say so myself, I am very satisfied with the end result. How well the book has turned out, though, I will naturally leave it up to the reader to judge!

Stephen James Walker
November 2022

About The Author

Stephen James Walker has authored or co-authored an average of one book per year since the early 1990s, many of them about the BBC's acclaimed *Doctor Who* series. *Wartime* is his thirty-second title.

He has a BSc (Hons) degree in Applied Physics from University College London, and his many other interests include cult TV, film noir, vintage crime fiction, Laurel and Hardy and an eclectic mix of soul, jazz, R&B and other popular music. Between July 1983 and March 2005 he acted as an adviser to successive Governments, responsible for policy on a range of issues relating mainly to individual employment rights.

His working time is now taken up by his writing projects and by his role as co-owner and director of Telos Publishing. He lives in Kent with his wife and family.

THE DÆMONS OF DEVIL'S END
Sam Stone, David J Howe, Raven Dane, Jan Edwards, Suzanne Barbieri and Debbie Bennett; with special picture 'Dossier' by Andrew-Mark Thompson

Olive Hawthorne is the sole guardian of the sleepy village of Devil's End. She protects the world from the incursion of demons, vampires, aliens and all manner of otherworldly creatures. But she is getting old … and they keep coming … This is the story of Olive's life. From her earliest days, through teenage years, middle age, and now old age. Tales of her adventures with monsters and evil … forever battling against the forces of darkness … and forever seeking to keep the world safe.

SIL AND THE DEVIL SEEDS OF ARODOR
Philip Martin

Sil is worried, very worried, which doesn't keep his reptilian skin in the best condition! Confined in a cold detention cell on the Moon, awaiting a deportation hearing for trial over drugs offences on Earth, he faces a death sentence if the application is successful and he is found guilty. And his employers at the Universal Monetary Fund aren't pleased either. Not at all. As time runs out and friends desert him, Sil must use all of his devious, vile, underhanded, ruthless and amoral business acumen to survive. Can he possibly slime his way out of this one?

DÆMOS RISING
David J Howe

Kate Lethbridge-Stewart is summoned by an old friend, Douglas Cavendish, to help him with a problem he has with ghosts and voices in his head. But when Kate arrives, she finds more than she expected. Aided by a time-traveller from the future, Kate must outwit both the ancient race of Daemons, and the Sodality, a Human cult-like organisation from the future, which is intent on gaining control over time.

MINDGAME
David J Howe

Sontaran Field-Major Sarg, Draconian Colonel Eskon and a Human mercenary who cannot remember her name have nothing in common ... that is until they are each snatched from their everyday lives to do battle in an alien arena on an asteroid suspended in the void! With a massive clash of cultures looming, can they each settle their differences and work together to defeat the alien intelligence which is trying to pit them against each other ...?

And then, once returned to their own times and places, can they continue as they were before, or has the experience changed them all?

FICTION ORIGINALS

HELEN MCCABE

THE PIPER TRILOGY
1: Piper
2: The Piercing
3: The Codex

SIMON CLARK
Humpty's Bones
The Fall

DAVID J HOWE
Talespinning
Horror collection of stories, short novels and more

RAVEN DANE

THE MISADVENTURES OF CYRUS DARIAN
Steampunk Adventure Series
1: Cyrus Darian And The Technomicron
2: Cyrus Darian And The Ghastly Horde
3: Cyrus Darian And The Wicked Wraith

Death's Dark Wings
Stand alone alternative history novel

Absinthe & Arsenic
Horror and fantasy short story collection

The Darkness Within: Final Cut
Science fiction horror novel

GRAHAM MASTERTON
The Djinn
The Wells Of Hell
Rules of Duel (With William S Burroughs)
The Hell Candidate

DAWN G HARRIS
Diviner
Supernatural horror thriller

FREDA WARRINGTON
Nights of Blood Wine
Vampire horror short story collection

TANITH LEE
Blood 20
20 vampire stories through the ages

Death Of The Day
Standalone crime novel

Tanith Lee A-Z
An A-Z collection of short fiction

STEPHEN LAWS
Spectre

SOLOMON STRANGE
The Haunting of Gospall

RHYS HUGHES
Captains Stupendous
Steampunk adventure novel

PAUL LEWIS
Small Ghosts
Horror novella

PAUL FINCH
Cape Wrath & The Hellion
Terror Tales of Cornwall ed. Paul Finch
Terror Tales of Northwest England ed. Paul Finch
Terror Tales of the Home Counties ed. Paul Finch
Terror Tales of the Scottish Lowlands ed. Paul Finch
Terror Tales of the West Country ed. Paul Finch

If you have enjoyed this book and would like more information about other TELOS titles, then check the website below.

TELOS PUBLISHING
www.telos.co.uk

WATCH THE ORIGINAL DRAMA

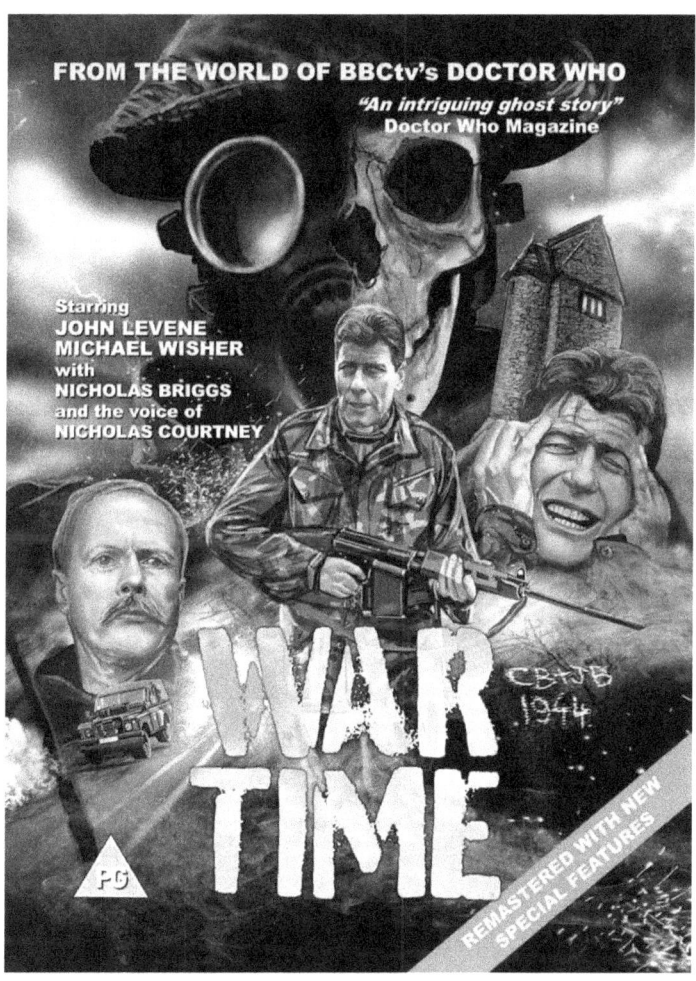

FROM THE WORLD OF BBCtv's DOCTOR WHO

"An intriguing ghost story"
Doctor Who Magazine

Starring
JOHN LEVENE
MICHAEL WISHER
with
NICHOLAS BRIGGS
and the voice of
NICHOLAS COURTNEY

WAR TIME

CB+JB 1944

PG

REMASTERED WITH NEW SPECIAL FEATURES

AVAILABLE FROM
www.timetraveltv.com